a breviary of fire

a breviary of fire

MARIE BRENNAN

BOOK VIEW CAFE

First published 2020 by Book View Café Publishing Cooperative.
304 S. Jones Blvd. Ste# 2906
Las Vegas, Nevada 89107
http://bookviewcafe.com

Print edition 2024
ISBN 978-1-63632-245-2

"This is How" was first published in *Strange Horizons*, 2019. "Serpent, Wolf, and Half-Dead Thing" was first published in *Bubble Off Plumb*, ed. K.G. Finfrock, Sarah Kalin, and Dan Kalin, 2018. "The Waking of Angantyr" was first published in *Heroic Fantasy Quarterly* #2, 2009. "Silence, Before the Horn" was first published in *Jabberwocky* #1, 2005. "Daughter of Necessity" was first published in *Tor.com*, 2014. "Your Body, My Prison, My Forge" was first published in *On Spec* #124, 2023. "For the Fairest" was first published in *Son and Foe* #1, 2005. "The Wives of Paris" was first published in *Mythic Delirium* 0.1, 2013. "The *Me* of Perfect Sight" was first published in *NewMyths* #58, 2022. "The Gospel of Nachash" was first published in *Clockwork Phoenix 3*, 2010. "Salt Feels No Pain" was first published in *Paradox* #13, 2009. "At the Heart of Each Pearl" was first published in *Sunday Morning Transport*, 2023. "Centuries of Kings" was first published in *Neverland's Library*, ed. Rebecca Lovatt and Roger Bellini, 2014. "The Old Woman and the Tea" was first published in *Daily Science Fiction*, 2021. "Ghost and Fox" was first published in *Shapers of Worlds II*, ed. Edward Willett, 2021. "Speak to the Moon" was first published in *The Magazine of Fantasy and Science Fiction*, 2021.

Contents

Foreword

There are five basic schools of thought on the topic of author commentary in a short story collection: 1) put it all together at the front; 2) all together at the back; 3) individually before each story; 4) individually after each story; and 5) don't bother.

For the ebook editions of these collections, I can leverage the format to facilitate multiple approaches, by linking to the notes at the end of each story while collecting the notes themselves at the end of the book. Alas, dead trees are not so flexible, which means I have to pick. You will find all the story notes following the Afterword, and can time your reading of them as you choose.

This collection contains sixteen stories, all of them based in some fashion on sources from folklore or mythology. They are divided into four groupings based on origin—Germanic, Greco-Roman, West Asian, and East Asian—and range in length from over six thousand words to a mere one hundred and seventy. I hope you enjoy them!

GERMANIC

This Is How

This is how a valravn is made:

A child dies. Lost in the woods, he curls up at the base of an ancient oak, and never rises again. Or she falters in the snow, lying down for a moment by the side of the road, just a moment to rest her eyes. Or, starving and alone, he weeps for someone to help him—but no one does.

A raven comes. Pecking, tearing, red blood on a black beak. Not eyes, as some tales would have it, but the cold red blood of the child's heart, chilled and stopped by death.

A child falls. A raven feeds. A valravn flies away.

This is how a valravn dies:

A noble warrior faces the ravenous foe. Bright steel against dark, bright armor against dark, and if he is quick enough and strong enough, he cuts the creature down. Where once a malevolent raven knight stood, there lies now the body of a bird, wings spread wide and still.

Or a woman catches a black-winged bird and pierces its breast with a pin of purest gold. The beak that once feasted on a child's corpse opens in a silent cry; the heart that beat with a child's blood stutters once and stops.

Or in a frozen wood a man kneels before the raven knight. He neither pleads for his life, nor fights to end the one that threatens his. A flash of shadow, a spatter of blood across the snow, and the man falls.

It will be a long time before the valravn realizes that he too died that day.

This is how a valravn weakens:

In small ways at first. Blood tastes less sweet; pleas for mercy ring slightly out of tune. When he takes human form his skin itches, as if something is crawling beneath it. When he takes raven form it feels wrong.

A valravn does not sleep. But when he sits alone, as human knight or scavenger bird, watching the stars and the moon and the blood-stained sunset, his mind is disturbed. The silence within is filled with murmurs he cannot quite make out. A valravn is not a person, to be troubled by hopes or fears or memories of the past. Yet he remembers: first in flashes, then in long, uneasy reveries, from which he wakes with the sense that someone was speaking to him. But he cannot remember what the voice said.

In place of silence, there is noise. In place of purity, there is doubt.

In place of the valravn, there is a creature that has begun to feel.

This is how a valravn falters:

He lets someone go.

A child. A girl, running along a path between two fields, hurrying home before night falls. The raven knight lands before her, a winged black shape plummeting into a tall figure of black steel, and she drops the bundle of firewood she is carrying. She doesn't shriek, this one, though her moon-wide eyes say she recognizes what he is. If she runs he will chase her, cut her down where she flees and drink her heart's blood on the banks of the nearby stream. If she does not run, he will cut her down where she stands and drink her heart's blood here between two fields.

Except he doesn't. She stands there, shivering, and he raises his blade and he does not strike. They stand there until the sun sets and the stars come out, until the waning sickle of the moon rises as if to reap what the valravn will not. By the end of the night she is swaying and exhausted, and when she closes her eyes for a too-long blink he is gone, black feathers vanishing into the darkness before dawn.

She picks up her bundle with shaking hands and staggers the rest of the way home.

This is how a valravn fights:

With claws and beak, with a sword of dark steel, and with all the malice of his corrupted heart.

Claws and beak and sword are no use against the voice inside his head, the voice of the man he killed.

Not the first. Nor the last. But this one was different—was, and is. They all live on within the valravn, the spirits of those he's slain; like a fox with her tails, they mark him as old and worthy of fear. No tail, though, has ever given a fox such trouble.

This one, he thinks, was a mistake.

I am sorry. The man's final words, on his knees in the snow. Odd words, for someone about to die. But he said them with such sincerity.

That sincerity rings through the valravn's hollow bones, an echo that will not let him rest. Sorrow has leached the savor from the blood of his prey. Compassion has formed an uncomfortable harmony with their pleas. Three words froze him on the path between the fields: *I am sorry.* As if he would apologize to the girl before he killed her.

Not *his* words. The words of the man he slew. A good man, filled with charity and mercy, temperance and kindness, who even in death refuses to be silent.

The solution is easy. Release that soul, and the valravn will be at peace once more.

But there is cruelty in the cold heart's blood of a child who died lost and alone. It is the cruelty of nature twisted to her harshest face, and it is what transforms an ordinary raven to a raven of the slain. A cat may let her prey run for a time before she catches it again, but not a valravn. He keeps what he kills, and will not let the man's soul go.

The next time he finds a child, he leaves the body in pieces, scattered across the daisies of the meadow.

This is how a valravn breaks:

In horror, in anguish, in grief.

He gathers up the scattered pieces from the stained carpet of daisies, as if he can stitch them back together again. But the force that transformed him gave him armor and a sword, not a needle and thread. He can kill, but he cannot heal.

He remembers healing.

He remembers gentle hands, cool water and a soft cloth to wipe the blood away. He remembers tearing a loaf of bread in two, and pressing one half into shaking, weakened hands; he remembers giving the other half away later, to a mother with an infant, and sleeping that night with his belly cold but his heart warm.

He remembers life instead of death. Soft voices instead of screams. Eyes wide with gratitude instead of fear.

But he also remembers killing, again and again, without mercy. Many, many deaths, but not too many to count, because their souls live on within him. He relives those moments in pitiless detail, the good man's soul grieving for each and every one.

What breaks him is the kindness, the compassion, the boundless heart that has room within it even for him. A creature born of death and abandonment, nature's heartless acts, should be beyond mercy. That is not what a valravn is *for*.

I am sorry. The man knew what a valravn was, long before the black-armored knight stood before him. And when he met one, that man grieved for the child who had died, for the raven who had unwittingly drunk the cold heart's blood. For what they had become.

That soul is there, too, buried beneath the rest.

The weight is too great for the valravn to bear. He curls up in his human form and screams; he cannot endure this shape, so much like the people he has killed. In raven form he huddles into himself, head beneath one wing, pecking desperately at his own breast as if his beak were a pin of gold. If there were a brave knight present he would spread his arms and welcome the shining blade.

There is no knight. There is only himself, and the soul of the good man, and all those the valravn has killed.

This is how a valravn changes:

One by one, he lets them go.

The souls drift upward like motes of light, but before that they tear free of him like his own bones coming out. Young and old, male and female, brave and angry and screaming in terror. They do not forgive him, even when he lets them go. They curse him as they depart. And the pain goes on and on, always more bones to rip out, more sins to remember. The snow around him turns red with blood, a stain becoming a carpet becoming a great frozen pool, stretching outward through the wood.

Soul after soul after soul, until only two remain.

Then he stops.

This is how a valravn fears:

Never once, in all his existence. From the moment he lifts his beak, gleaming with a child's heart's blood, fear never touches him. He sees it, feeds on it, relishes its delicate taste, but never lets it strike him.

Until now, when he hovers on the brink. Two paths lie before him, and both, he fears, lead to damnation.

Release the child, and die at last, completing the death that began when he slew the good man—but that man's soul will die with him.

Or release the man, and return to what he was when he

began, a dead child's soul in the body of a raven—but the warmth within him will be gone.

And without that warmth, what is he but a valravn? A killer without mercy. A creature that knows no kindness. He may remember what he has done, but the spark that began it will have flickered out, and the ashes it leaves behind cannot burn. He will begin again, repeating all his sins of before, and the thought of that terrifies him.

Or a third path. Stay as he is. But the fire burns too hot for that; he *wants* to release the two souls that remain. He knows now what goodness is, and cannot reach that star while he holds two innocents trapped. Without them, though—without one or the other—

The good man is silent. He has wisdom, but no answers. There are no tales of a choice like this.

The child. The man. Neither.

Death. Damnation. Suffering.

A choice.

This is how a valravn chooses:

He lets the good man go.

This is how a valravn is remade:

In mercy, in justice, in repentance.

The soul of the good man flies free, and there is no pain as it goes. The raven is left alone with the soul of the child who died alone—but not like it was before.

Where there used to be a raven, where there used to be a dark-armored knight, a child stands in the snow.

He looks at his hands in wonder, then touches one to his breast where a beak once pierced and tore. The skin there is soft and unmarked—and it is warm.

Take fire from fire, and fire remains behind. It will continue to burn as long as it has fuel: the desire to do good instead of ill, to make amends for the sins of the past. He has freed the souls he wronged, and the one that remains is no victim of his. What killed that child, what kills all such children, is something else.

Perhaps, he thinks, he can help change that.

The air rustles, and black wings spread. But this time, their feathers are tipped with gold.

A child rises. A raven repents. A goðravn flies away.

Serpent, Wolf, and Half-Dead Thing

WITH HIS FANGS still buried in the thick meat of his own tail, the great serpent says, "I wondered when you would come."

She scowls at him with the dead half of her face. Her tangled, knotted hair floats weed-like around her, but the harsh croak of her voice is as clear as if she stood in the open air. "What do you know, old snake?"

It's cold down here, in the depths of the sea that encircles the world. He is sluggish with the chill, but his mind is more awake than she's ever seen it, since the day they flung him out here. Something has wakened him. "Know?" the serpent asks, thoughtfully. "Many things. There is wisdom here the Allfather has not: the secret movements of the hafgufa and lyngbakr, the shape of stone that has never seen light, the pattern of the currents of the deep. This wisdom is mine alone."

Her lip curls in disgust. He's grown strange, this past age— from the chill, the darkness, the loneliness of his exile? She hardly cares. Her visits are rare, and growing rarer; she stirs less and less often from her own lonely realm. What do the three of them have to say to each other, or to anyone?

Until now. "I saw the light dim," he admits after a thoughtful pause. "And I heard the beasts of the sea weep—a thing never heard before."

One enormous golden eye regards her. How much *does* he know? She says, "They wept for the death of light."

The tip of his tail shifts, rippling the water. Ships will shudder in the waves high above. "Father's work," the serpent says.

Of course. Who else would devise such a malicious trick? "And he is punished for it," she tells her monstrous brother. "Bound beneath the earth, with venom dripping upon his face." One trick too many. They've forgiven his evils before, but not now. Not with the Allfather's own son struck down, pierced with mistletoe, his shining beauty dimmed by death.

Another ripple, that in a human creature might have been a shrug. But they are not human, none of them—not even she, for all that she has the look. Their shapeshifter father takes any form he chooses, but their mother is a giant, and gave birth to monsters.

Monsters who could not be trusted in the world of men, nor gods neither. And so the gods flung this one out into the sea, where he grew beyond even the ken of his mother's race. The serpent says, "It matters not to me. Norns wove our fates before they began, and the fates of the nine worlds."

This is what her brother has fallen to, here in the depths of the sea. Apathy. He may have wisdom, but to no purpose. He does not care what their father has done.

Even the brief wakefulness it brought is fading. "What will you do, old snake?"

Drowsy amusement fills the eye she can see. "Poison the sky. Slay a god. Then die. But the time has not yet come."

The time when he will take his fangs from out his great tail and uncoil his length from around the world of men. The final battle, the twilight of the gods. Many know the fates they will find there. She imagines it to be a cruel thing, knowing one's own end so clearly—but not half so cruel as ignorance. The Allfather claims her people will be there when the battle comes, fighting at her father's side; but of her he has said nothing.

The eye is drooping shut. Her brother is subsiding once more, back into the half-dreaming sleep that consumes the span of his life. She watches with contempt. This is his kingdom, beyond even the reach of the sea-god, but he cannot be troubled to rule it.

When at last she turns to go, she thinks she hears a whisper from behind her. "Farewell, sister."

But when she glances back, her brother is fast asleep.

The black surface of the lake barely ripples as she passes over it to the heather-strewn island beyond. No one comes here, even less than to the depths of the sea; this was a sacred place once, but now is haunted by the howls of the wolf.

He thrashes when he sees her. No apathy, not here; his hatred only burns hotter with every passing age. It's a hatred he shares with all, but not equally. She has a relatively small portion of it as such things go.

In part because she is the only one who will take the sword from within his jaws. The hilt rests on his lower gums, and the point gouges a bloody hole in the upper. Though smaller than their serpentine brother, he is still the mightiest wolf the nine worlds have ever seen. Little wonder the gods grew to fear him.

She reaches in, grasps the leather-bound hilt with her living hand, pries the sword free. The wolf spits blood into the river of saliva that flows from his mouth. They call that river Hope; it's fitting that its waters should sometimes run red.

"I bring news," she says.

Golden eyes glare at her. It's the one thing all three of them share, the only mark of kinship among them. Their mother does not have such eyes. Perhaps their father does—but who can tell, behind the lies?

"Unbind me," the wolf snarls, as he always does.

She does not even bother to look. She knows well the silken ribbon that binds him, woven of six impossible things, beyond even his strength to break; she knows the fetter that leads from it, the slab to which the fetter is bound, the stone that anchors it all to the earth. Unlike their mother, she is no giant. She can move none of it.

Instead she surprises herself by echoing the serpent's words. "The time has not yet come."

The wolf snaps at her arm, so that she has to lift the sword to warn him back. He would have claimed more than a single hand, had they not wedged his jaws open. "The time will come when I escape my bonds. Let it be *now*. I will feast upon them all, and howl my victory to the desolation."

He hears only as much of his doom as he wishes to. That is not how it will go. He will die, just as the serpent will; his mouth will be torn apart, so he can howl no more. It is a bloody fate that has been woven for them, when they were but new-born.

For two of them, at least.

She says, "I came to tell you that Father is bound."

The wolf bares his teeth, slaver dripping from his jaws. "What do I care? *I* have been bound for ages. If he shares my fate, it's only fitting. Why should any of us walk free?"

The binding upon him will not break before the end of the world; that knowledge is the only thing that keeps her from stepping back. This is the hate he reserves for her, that she, alone of the three, can go where she wills. It's a freedom she rarely enjoys, and he hates her all the more for that. But there is no welcome for her anywhere outside her realm, not even in the company of her kin, and certainly not among the gods.

Her lupine brother, though, is not the only one who bears hatred in his heart. "Why should any of us have enjoyed the warmth of the gods' own halls?" she spits. "I am not the one who played the faithful hound, accepting scraps from my master's hand, all for the hope that they would accept me among them. That they would *love* me."

She can scarcely hear her own words in the end, drowned out by the wolf's fury. This is what he despises above all: not her, nor the gods, nor even the one who betrayed his trust, but himself, for having given that trust to begin with. He played their games, let them place fetters on his limbs, because he hoped it would earn him a place among them. And the one he called friend, the only one brave enough to come near him, promised it would be so.

Perhaps the gods also deceived their fellow. His honesty is renowned as much as his courage, even now, when the stump of his wrist proclaims his lie. It hardly matters. That lost hand rots in the wolf's belly, and her brother will never trust again.

A necessary thread, dyed black with blood. The wolf could never be their faithful hound; they knew that when he was still a pup, and that is why they bound him. Their binding created his hatred—and thus is the tapestry woven.

She chooses her moment with care. When the wolf lunges against his silken chain, hoping to claim a taste of her flesh, she thrusts the sword once more into place. Fresh blood springs free as it digs once more into his gums. It is necessary; the guardian of the gods sees all, and he must see the wolf as he was before she came. But she feels a touch of pleasure, too, as she forces the blade into her brother's mouth. He knows what she never will: what it is like to dwell among the gods. To pretend, however briefly, that she belongs with them.

With the wolf's howls once more wordless in her ears, she turns her back on the river Hope and leaves her brother to his fate.

The earth bucks like a horse fighting to throw its rider, like the sea heaving in a storm. She waits until it calms before she approaches the mouth of the cave.

Darkness envelops her as if welcoming her home. But this is not her realm, and she is not welcome here.

Her father's wife makes that very plain. The goddess sits patiently by her bound husband's side, hands clasping a wide, shallow bowl. Above waits a snake; his venom hisses as it strikes the basin, and foul smoke wisps into the air. Beneath lies the maker of mischief, the thief from giants, the great liar himself— her father.

His breath comes quick, and his hands still clench and flex as if to purge the pain. Red weals mark his face where the venom struck, in the moment when his wife turned aside to empty the bowl. It was his convulsions she felt a moment before, shaking all the earth, so that men everywhere might remember his torment, and his crime.

It will end only when the world does. When he rises from his chains to fight against the gods, and those who were once his companions.

Perhaps it is better to have always been alone. She cannot betray, when she has no friends. And she cannot be betrayed.

She looks to the goddess and says, "I will hold it for a time."

Her father's wife hesitates. This is not her mother; what sons the goddess bore have fallen to their own fates. The guts of one now bind his father to the stone, bloody ropes transformed to iron bands, that will endure until the end of time. And she hates the children the giantess bore.

But her vigil is long, and the goddess loses nothing by letting another bear her burden for a while.

The stone bowl weighs heavy in mismatched hands—one living flesh, one dead claw. She waits until the goddess is gone, and then she speaks.

"Why?"

Her father lets out a ragged breath, something like a laugh. "You look well. On the right side, at least. Let your hair fall across the left; otherwise you will never get a husband."

The bowl trembles. She wants to fling its contents into his face, hear him scream in pain. But then the goddess would return, and there is more she must say first.

"I tried to save you," she tells her father. The words have to be forced out, a harsher rasp than usual. "When their messenger came…I was willing to give him up." The light of the gods, the Allfather's brightest child. He lit her gloomy hall like the sun, turning its chill, sleeting rains to showers of gold. But there need be no vengeance for one who is not dead, and so she promised that if all the world wept for him, she would let him go.

And all the world wept—except one.

This time her father's laugh is stronger. "They speak wrongly who say that because the heart lies on the left, yours must be a black and rotted thing."

Always mocking. She wonders if he knows how to do anything else. Gritting her teeth, she asks again. "Why? Why did you kill him, why did you disguise yourself and refuse to mourn?"

"Perhaps I did it for you."

She spits a curse at him.

"No," he agrees, in the same friendly tone. "I didn't think you would believe it. Though that would be a wondrous gift, would it not? A companion in your dark and freezing realm. The sort of thing a loving father might do for his lonely daughter."

"You have never been a loving father." But she does not bother to dispute the other.

He sighs, and his eyes move restlessly, as if already bored with the view: the bowl, her hands, and the stone roof above. "The tapestry is woven, its threads long since spun. This was always the place I would come to."

"And so you ran to meet it? The one crime he could never forgive—and when it seemed you might be spared his wrath, you made sure to seal your doom. But if this was always where you would come, why did it have to be by that road? Why help fate in its work?"

The light in this cave is dim; his eyes hold no color, only darkness. But she sees something in them that might be amusement, or pity, or both. "You don't care what I've done, or why. Your real question is more interesting: you want to know how to face your *own* fate."

She shakes her head, and the tangles fall forward, masking the living side of her face, leaving him only the sight of death. "My fate is secret, known only to the norns."

He shrugs as much as he can, with stones beneath his shoulders and hips and knees, and the guts of his own slaughtered son binding him in place. "Whether you know it or not, your fate is fixed. And so you wonder whether our choices even matter. Whether *your* choices matter."

"Do they?"

Her father smiles. Despite the red weals, despite his prison, despite that he is the greatest traitor the gods have ever known, she still sees it there in his smile: the sly charm, beguiling her against her will, whispering that even if she can't trust him, she still wants to listen. No wonder they tolerated him for so long.

"Of course," he says. "Our choices are the only thing that matters. Whether you cringe from your fate or embrace it, you end up in the same place. You might as well keep your pride."

She stares at him, and he grins back, until the goddess returns. Then she leaves him to his torment, knowing she will not see him again before the end of the world.

Her hall is dark and cold again. Her bright companion she has banished from her sight, for she cannot bear his company. Not for more than a few moments at a time. This has been her realm for too long, since the Allfather cast her down here to rule over the inglorious dead. She is used to the shadows and chill.

To her belong the forgotten ones, those not fortunate enough to perish in battle and thereby join the Allfather's host. His dead pass their time in feasting and fighting; hers enjoy no such comforts, and all for the sin of unremarkable death. She does not wonder why they will fight against him in the end.

She wonders instead about herself. What deeds she will do, when that end comes.

The gods fear all three of them: serpent, wolf, and half-dead thing. She understands the first two, but not the third. What doom awaits her, what evil will she commit? For now she is a queen, ruling over her great hall of frozen mist, and that is more than her brothers have; but in the end she will have less. The dead will go to fight for her father, and what happens then, only the Allfather knows.

So she cannot take refuge in her serpentine brother's uncaring patience. Nor can she, like the wolf, reach with hungry jaws for the blood of her foes. She cannot even follow her father's advice, to keep her pride and embrace her fate.

Our choices are the only thing that matters.

To choose blindly…

Her mismatched hands tighten on the arms of her throne.

To *choose.*

Half living, half dead. Half of this realm, and half not. If she had dwelt all this time among the gods…

Their actions create their fates, a net that none can escape. Yet if her fate is to choose, then why would the Allfather send her among the dead, to live lonely and cold, with no cause to love anyone at all? Not the gods, nor the monsters that are her kin. But it could have been different, had they not cast her out.

Perhaps he fears what he does not know. And just as she cannot understand what it is to know one's own fate, the Allfather cannot understand what it is to choose.

Perhaps all of this is mere delusion: a story she has spun for herself, like the neglected child who pretends her real parents will come for her someday. A scrap of warmth against the cold. Her fate might be as fixed as anyone else's.

But she might as well keep her pride.

Hel straightens on her throne, and considers her choice.

The Waking of Angantyr

BETWEEN ONE STROKE of his hoe and the next, the farmer saw her.

The dying sun made her into a black silhouette, tall against the fiery sky. She paused for a moment at the top of the hill, then came his way with determined strides. He went on hoeing—little enough time left, before sunset—but kept a wary eye on her. Strangers had no reason to be here.

When she came within speaking distance, he stopped.

Her face was scratched and dirty, her blonde hair hanging in tangled ropes. With a pack slung over one shoulder, she looked like a vagabond, but her bearing said otherwise. She radiated purpose. The farmer gripped his hoe more firmly.

Her eyes fixed on him, winter-blue against her grimy skin, and she spoke.

"Am I on Sámsey?"

"That you are," the farmer said, not relaxing. She didn't look like the survivor of a wreck. Kicked off some passing ship, maybe. "Where were you headed for?"

"Here," she said. For all her height, the farmer realized, she was barely fully grown; beneath the dirt, her face was young. "I didn't know if I'd landed in the right place."

The farmer stared. "You were coming *here*? Sweet sun, what for? There's nothing on Sámsey but farms and ghosts!"

A twisted smile passed across her face—the smile of someone who has seen her fate and must either laugh or go mad. "So I've been told."

"You'll be needing shelter," the farmer said. Stranger she

might be, but she seemed a harmless kind of crazy, and it was bad luck not to be kind to lunatics. "It's not far to sunset, and you don't want to be out at night. I don't know what possessed you to come to Sámsey, girl, but take my word—this isn't any kind of place for sane people. Most everybody has left. *I'd* leave, if I could."

She shook her head. "Thanks, but what I really need is directions. I'm looking for a burial mound."

"Sámsey's covered with them," he said. That was the whole problem.

"A specific one." She turned her head to gaze across the undulating ground of the island. "Thirteen men lie buried in it. A recent mound, built not more than fifteen years ago."

The farmer flinched. He didn't think she was looking at him, but she came alive at his reaction, moving suddenly closer. He retreated, holding his hoe like a defense. "Where is it?" she asked.

He shook his head, knowing already that he would lose this argument. Ragged as she was, she looked like one of *those* people— the sort who answered to a code that had nothing to do with common sense. But he had to try. "You don't want to go there, girl. This whole island's haunted, and that mound more than most. Come nightfall, it'll open up, and the flames will rise, and you don't want to be outside when that happens."

"Where is it?" she repeated, her voice iron-hard. As he had known she would.

Against his will, his arm rose to point. He knew the mound; everyone on Sámsey did. It lay on the island's southeastern edge, not far from where they stood.

She began walking that way immediately.

"How are you going to know which one it is?" the farmer called after her desperately.

"The ghosts will tell me!" she shouted back. "They brought me this far."

⁂

Hervor found the mound shortly before sunset. It was easy to spot; thirteen men required a large barrow. She needed no ghostly voices to tell her that.

But they'd told her many other things. They had whispered to her in her sleep since childhood, murmurs of battle and betrayal and thirteen men murdered. That was how she knew their number. Finding out that they lay buried on Sámsey had not been so easy—ghosts, it seemed, were better at counting than geography—but she persevered. Because while she'd gotten used to dead men's voices in her sleep, lately they'd begun speaking to her in broad daylight. From that point on, it was clear: find them and silence them, or go mad.

She dumped the contents of her ragged pack onto the ground. Bones and leather and gleaming white stones tumbled out; she left them where they lay and pried an egg-sized rock out of the earth. Then she began to wander, ranging outward from the burial mound in growing arcs until she found a small hole, barely visible in the grass. From one pocket she produced an apple core, which she tossed down a few paces from the hole.

Then she crouched and waited.

Soon a twitching pink nose emerged from the burrow, followed a moment later by the rest of a skinny brown rabbit. The animal hesitated. Hervor did not move. It hopped forward, paused, then darted for the apple core. The instant it stopped, Hervor threw her rock.

The furry body pitched over sideways. Hervor ran forward and grabbed it; the thing was only stunned, not dead, and it struggled as she bundled it into the tattered end of her shirt. The squirming was a nuisance, but she needed the rabbit alive.

Not for much longer, though. The sun was almost down.

Hervor returned to the burial mound, stuffed the rabbit into her now-empty pack, and began to lay everything out.

The rough square of leather she staked to the ground with four bones, one at each corner. Her hands shook; this was *drauðr*, blood magic, and she'd heard enough tales of what could go wrong. There was a reason *drauðr* was spoken of only in whispers—when it was spoken of at all. Getting the old woman to talk about it hadn't been easy.

But the crone's determination was nothing against Hervor's. This was the only way she would ever have peace.

So she steadied her hands and drew a circle on the leather, taking care to make the line solid and thick. In a few minutes, it would be the only thing keeping her safe. Best to be sure.

The circle drawn, she placed thirteen pale stones inside it, pale like the dead. One for each voice, each ghost, and a line to hold them in when the time came.

Madness, every bit of this. But she had only two choices: go on, or give up. And she could not give up.

Hervor laid her knife down on the leather. Then she dragged the rabbit from the bag, where it was trying to chew its way free. She held the squirming animal in her arms and waited for the last sliver of sun to vanish below the horizon.

In the peculiar light of dusk, the barrow opened up.

There were no doors. The ground did not shift. Hervor was looking straight ahead at the grass, and then suddenly she saw through it to the chamber inside, where thirteen men sat cross-legged, their swords leaning against their shoulders, chill blue flames dancing around them and over their skin.

Their voices rose in her mind, whispers familiar from her earliest memories.

blood

                                        betrayal

MURDER

                                                lying cold

rivers of blood

                        and they're beyond our reach…

They sat in two ranks, six on a side, and the thirteenth faced her from the depths of the mound. The flames leapt higher around him, throwing his corpse-white face into hideous relief; his eyes glowed with the same blue light. He alone faced her, but he could neither see nor hear her. Not yet.

Hervor pinned the struggling hindquarters of the rabbit between her knees, stretched its neck over the leather square, and slit its throat.

The blood fountained over her knees and hands and the leather before her, drenching the white stones in red. For a moment it pooled in the center of the circle, unnaturally; then it drained into the thirteen stones, which began to glow with a sullen, bloody light. The four bones shone cold blue in response, the same blue as the barrow's flames.

The body of the rabbit fell to the ground, drained, and then Hervor spoke the invocation the old woman had taught her, using the names gleaned from so many nights of dreams.

> "Wake thou, Angantyr—　　Hervor wakes you.
> Son of Arngrím,　　son of Grím,
> son of Hergrím,　　hear me speak.
> Rise from your grave;　　give me your words.
>
> Sons of Angantyr,　　see me before you!
> Hervard, Hjórvard,　　Hrani, Barri,
> clad all in mail,　　I call you forth.
> Death holds you not;　　I open the door.
>
> Reifnir, Tindr,　　Tóki, Bófi,
> white in your barrow,　　weapons in hand—
> Búi, Haddingr,　　Brami, Saemingr!
> Feast on the blood　　brought here for you.
>
> Angantyr, warrior,　　wake to my call,
> with blood and bone　　I bid you hear me.
> Wake thou, Angantyr,　　answer my voice,
> from the barrow-mound　　I beckon you forth!"

The thirteenth ghost stood.

Despite her determination, Hervor flinched back. In his hand he held a sword, unsheathed: Tyrfing, the blade famed in all the tales of Angantyr. The old woman had said he could not harm her—none of them could, not with the charcoal line holding them in—but Hervor found it hard to trust. Was the sword ghostly, or real?

But she had what she wanted; the ghosts, fed by the rabbit's blood, could hear her. She must not waste that. She must speak to them, if she wanted answers. If she wanted peace.

"You've haunted my sleep for years."

Vengeance.

They spoke the word together. Hervor expected their lips would move, that she would hear them with her ears, but no—their disembodied voices echoed in her head as they always had, inescapable and cold. They'd never spoken of vengeance before, in all their years of whispering, but she wasn't surprised. What else would murdered men want?

"Why are you in my dreams?" she asked.

Sváfa's daughter.

That came from the thirteenth ghost alone. Angantyr. His frost-blue eyes held Hervor pinned. She trembled under his gaze, but made herself ask, "How do you know my mother's name?" Maybe ghosts just knew things.

Maybe not.

Angantyr came forward two steps, each one shivering the ground. *Why do you call us from the cold earth?*

"To silence you," Hervor said. The words limped from her, not nearly as strong as she'd meant them to be. "I'm sick of hearing you in my sleep, let alone when I'm awake. You want vengeance? Tell me who killed you."

Two eagles flew against us, the ghost of Angantyr murmured. *Battle in the sky. I will say no more.*

Hervor gritted her teeth. They could not haunt her for so many years, and then answer her only in riddles. "The honor of Arngrím's mighty line has turned to dust, if Angantyr and his sons fear to speak their killers' names."

The other ghosts murmured, their words indistinguishable.

One by one their heads were turning to face her. At least they didn't stand. Hard enough to face Angantyr on his own.

Her insult, it seemed, struck home. *The eagles flew from the great lord's hall,* Angantyr said at last. *His retainer Hjálmar, and Orvar the wanderer. The first stood against me, and the second, my sons.*

Two. Two men alone had been the end of Angantyr and his twelve berserker sons. And now they demanded vengeance.

Hervor was young and strong, but she'd been raised a bondsmaid. Hers had been a life of washing and cooking, not war. Orvar had killed Angantyr's twelve sons; Hjálmar had killed Angantyr himself, who—the stories said—was greater than his sons together.

Living with the voices didn't look so bad, when compared with certain death.

But how could she say that, after coming so far?

The blood of my line burdened the earth, Angantyr's spectral voice said. *One alone bears it now.*

A cold touched Hervor that had nothing to do with the barrow's chill. "What did you say?" she whispered, through nerveless lips.

The ghost's eyes seared like ice. *Daughter of Sváfa: you bear my blood.*

She was shaking her head before she even realized it. Angantyr's wife had been Tofa, not Sváfa, and Sváfa was her mother; even he admitted that. She couldn't be his daughter.

As if no one had ever been sired out of wedlock before.

Thus the voices, the dreams, the haunting since childhood. Who else would they cry to for vengeance, when all their other kin were dead?

Vengeance she couldn't give them. Hjálmar and Orvar would carve her to pieces; she didn't stand a chance.

But that wasn't the point. Honor was the point. If she was born of Angantyr's blood, she was no common thrall, and that meant she could allow herself no common weakness. In truth, she'd left that life behind a year ago, when she fled to seek out the ghosts and silence them. She'd already begun walking the path that blood laid out for her—which meant that honor must be her guiding force, now. Honor, and fate.

The gods had spun the skein of her life long ago. She would die either way, fighting or not. Or so they said. But the abstract idea of fate had never been so sharply real.

Hervor closed her eyes, searching for the courage to speak. Her head dipped, and when she opened her eyes, she found herself looking at her hands, streaked with rabbit's blood. Too much to hope it would some day be replaced by Hjálmar's. But she clenched her teeth and dragged her chin upward, intending to meet her father's eyes and speak the words honor demanded of her.

Her gaze stopped on his sword. Tyrfing, a blade as famous as the man who bore it.

A pointless gesture, perhaps—but if she was doomed, she might as well do it right.

"Give me your sword, and I will avenge you."

Silence. No answering whisper, no call for blood.

Hervor raised her eyes to meet her father's, and found his face as cold and forbidding as winter itself.

You court your doom, Angantyr said. *Your sense abandons you, when you come to the barrow and call up the dead. The spectral fires encircle you; death's domain beckons you in. Flee to your ship. Leave us in peace.*

"*What* peace?" Hervor cried, angered by his sudden dismissal. "Your murders have kept you lingering for fifteen years. And I have lingered *with* you, hearing your voices—but I will hear no more. Fires do not frighten me, though hellish their source; I have come through worse to find you tonight. I will take Tyrfing, to seek out your foes."

The blade gleamed in Angantyr's hand. *Listen, my daughter— hear my words out! Tyrfing, my sword, shall bring you no joy. Cursed it was, when first it killed. Let it stay in my barrow, lest ruin it bring to all of your kin.*

"I have no kin for it to ruin! My father lies murdered; my brothers lie with him. What have I to lose?" Hervor's hands clenched into fists, her nails cutting her skin.

Sons, Angantyr replied. *Disaster will this blade bring to you and your children, though you prevail against Hjálmar and Orvar.*

Hervor's breath died in her throat.

Hear thou, daughter, the character of this blade.

Behind Angantyr, his sons rose and drew their swords.

Deadly the edges; each carries poison. It shines as the sun, when it is unsheathed; fierce is this light, it betrays you to foes. Tyrfing may never be unsheathed without causing the death of a man, and it may not be sheathed again unless blood lies warm upon it.

Hervor stared at the blade. Yes, the stories had hinted of this—but they were just stories. People always exaggerated. But she did not think her father did. She did not think he *could.*

Nor was he finished. *This doom does it bear, from the hand of the gods: Tyrfing shall be the cause of three dishonorable deaths. But it will never turn on you, and so long as you bear it, blades will not cut you. Think this not a blessing: disaster it will bring to your sons, though honor you regain.*

His words threatened Hervor's fragile self-control, her new-found determination and courage. Against her will, a tear slipped free of her eye, tracking through the dirt on her face. Doom her sons, or fail her duty. What kind of choice was that?

Return to your home, Angantyr said. *Reach not for such pain.*

Pain. Either way she turned, she could not escape it. Would she even live to bear sons, if the ghosts kept haunting her, their murders unanswered? Or would she die, driven mad by this burden? What legacy would she give her sons, having failed in her duty as Angantyr's last kin?

Frustration and despair swamped her, dragging her spirit down. Hervor fled them, curling in on herself, reaching deep within for the strength that set her on this path in the first place.

She reached for strength, and found anger.

Anger at the two who had murdered the kinsmen she'd never known, damning her to a life as a bondsmaid. Anger at the gods who had cursed the blade, damning innocents to suffer for it. Anger at—at *everyone,* from her father to the farmer who thought she should hide inside and hope for safety. She faced her doom either way, but if so....

If so, she would face it on her feet, and regain her family's honor. Whatever the price.

Hervor stood.

She stepped over the bloodstained leather, came forward until she reached the very edge of the flames that encircled the mound. They sank low at her approach. Angantyr stood before her, separated only by the veil of blue light.

"Let my sons fend for themselves," Hervor said, no hint of tremor in her voice. "I have no dread of the doom you name. Not ghosts, nor gods, nor the flames of hell frighten me. Give me your sword. I will seek out the warriors that slew you and your sons. My father and brothers will rest in their graves before I am done."

Behind Angantyr, the twelve brothers she had never known stood arrayed, their swords in hand. In their dead eyes she saw pride, but in her father's she saw sorrow.

"Give Tyrfing to me," Hervor said. "I will find my own fate."

The cold blue fire grew in intensity until she had to close her eyes against its brilliance. When it faded, she found herself standing at the very base of the grassy mound. Dawn light came from the eastern horizon; night had passed without her knowing.

The sun glinted off something at the top of the mound.

Tyrfing.

Hervor stood, trembling. The blade lay in the grass, there for the taking. A chance to find peace.

If she was lucky. If she was strong enough.

Hervor climbed to the top of the mound and picked up the sword. As she touched it, the blade began to shine with its own light, rivaling that of the sun.

Her sons would be born of an honorable line. Whatever their fate, they would face it on their own.

Silence, Before the Horn

IN THE END, we all chose sleep. Skuld was the first to go; they say she went to Svalbard, to the glaciers that never melt, and locked in ice she dreams the centuries away. Thrúth sleeps in stone, Hrist in the bole of an ancient tree. Brynhild chose fire, and left it once, but to fire she returned, immolating herself to escape a greater pain.

And I? I chose water. The gentle lap of waves on a lakeshore, in a distant land where I thought I would not be disturbed. We were tired, all of us, tired of choosing the slain, tired of the endless round of battle and death. We chose instead to sleep: a little death we granted to ourselves.

But my sleep did not last. A magician, a worker of charms, divined what lay beneath the surface of my lake. He served a warrior, and brought him there, and the warrior demanded my sword from me.

And I? I gave it up. Let another choose who would die. But a valkyrie, it seems, cannot renounce her nature so easily. Had he not taken my sword, he would have lived to great age, and his shining kingdom would have endured for generations to come. As it was, he died in battle: I chose him, and he was slain.

Perhaps he wanted it that way.

When he lay dying on the shore, he returned the sword to me. Twice his companions refused, but at his word they came a third time and flung the blade over the water. I caught it as it flew, one white-clad arm rising above the surface of the lake. I wonder what his companions made of that.

He carouses now in the Allfather's hall, waiting with the

others for the end that will come. Or he sleeps under a hill: a more dignified image. Either is true, or neither, or both. It does not matter. He waits, and will return.

And I? I wait as well. We cannot sleep forever. We will take our rest while we can, I in my lake, Skuld in ice, Brynhild in fire. We will rise when the horn sounds, and do battle, and die: a death chosen for us when time began.

GRECO-ROMAN

Daughter of Necessity

THE STRANDS THRUM faintly beneath her fingertips, like the strings of a lyre. Plain grey wool, held taut by the stone weights tied at the ends, awaiting her hand. She can feel the potential in the threads, the resonance. She has that much of the gift, at least.

But it is madness to think she can do more. It is *hubris*.

It is desperation.

Her maid stands ready with the bone pick. She takes it up, slides its point beneath the first thread, and begins to weave.

Antinoös will be the most easily provoked. He has no care for the obligations of a guest, the courtesy due to his host; he sees only the pleasures to be had in food and drink. If these are restricted, marred—the meat burnt, the wine thin, the grapes too soon consumed—then he will complain. And it will take but one poorly-phrased reassurance for his complaint to become more than mere words.

The guards will know to watch for this. When Antinoös draws his knife, they will be ready. Others will come to Antinoös' aid, of course; the tables will be knocked aside, the feast trampled underfoot, the rich treasures of the hall smashed to pieces.

Antinoös will not be the first to die, though. That will be Peisandros, who will fall with a guard's sword through his heart. After him, Klymenos, and then Pseras of the guards; then it will be a dozen, two score, three hundred and more dead, blood in a torrent, flames licking at the palace walls, smoke and death and devastation.

She drops the shuttle, shaking with horror. *No, no.* That was not how she meant it to go.

"My lady?" the maid asks, uncertain.

She almost takes up scissors and cuts her error away. Some fragment of wisdom stops her: that is not her gift, and to try must surely end in disaster. Instead she retrieves the shuttle, sends it back through without changing the shed. Unweaving the line that had been. "The pick," she commands, and her maid gives it to her in silent confusion. With a careful hand she lifts the warp threads, passes the shuttle through, reversing her move-ments from before. Undoing the work of hours with hours more, while her maid helps without understanding.

I must weave a funeral shroud, she had told them. She'd intended it to be for them. Not for all her city.

But the power was there: within her grasp, beyond her control.

She retires for the night, trembling, exhausted. Frightened. And exhilarated. When morning comes, all is as it was before, her problems unchanged, her desperation the same. Gathering her courage, she goes back to the loom.

Surely control may be learned.

After so many years enjoying the hospitality of the palace, the men will not be easily persuaded to leave. Frustration and failure will not do it; if those were sufficient, they would have departed long since. They stay on in perpetual hope of success, and will not leave until they believe that hope gone.

She will choose her tool with care. Eurymachos is renowned for his silver tongue; he will bend it to her chosen end. A dropped hint here, a frank conversation over too much wine there. Why should a man stay, when he believes another has claimed the place he intended to take? An elegant man, well-dressed and better-spoken than his rivals—and they will see the proof of it, when she bestows smiles upon him she denies to all others. For him, she will drape herself in rich cloth, adorn her ears and neck with gold. For him, she will play the coquette.

One by one, they will go. Grumbling, disappointed, a few vowing some revenge against Eurymachos for having stolen the place they thought to claim. But they will go, without a fight. Their numbers will dwindle: one hundred and eight, four score, two score, twelve. They will leave, and with each chamber emptied she will breathe more easily.

Until only one remains. Smiling, smooth-spoken Eurymachos, to whom she has shown much favor. *He* will not leave. For has she not made a promise to him, in the absence of her husband, whom all presume dead?

Too late, she will see that it has gone too far. He has coaxed from her words she never meant to speak, implications she cannot disavow. To do so would bring war, and the destruction she sought to avoid. She will have no choice but to acquiesce, for the sake of her people, for the sake of her son.

She will fail, and pay the price of that failure until the end of her days.

This time she is shaking with rage. To be so manipulated, so trapped…she would die before she allowed that to happen.

Or would she? After all, the future now hanging on the loom is her own creation. However undesirable, it is *possible*. She could not have woven it, were it not so.

Her maid waits at her shoulder. They have long since begun to tell tales, she knows, her maidservants whispering of their mistress' odd behavior. They think it only a tactic for delay, an excuse for avoiding the men. That, they whisper, is why she undoes her work each night, reclaiming her spent thread, only to start anew in the morning.

As reasons go, it is a good one. They need not know the rest of her purpose. If any hint of *that* reached the men, all hope of her freedom would be gone.

Night after night, fate after fate. She can only keep trying. Surely somewhere, in all the myriad crossings of the threads, there is a future in which all will be well.

Her son will ask again for stories of his father, and she will tell him what she knows. That the king was summoned to war, and he went; that many who sailed to the east never returned.

This time, Telemachos will not be content with the familiar tale. He will insist on hearing more. When she cannot satisfy him, he will declare his intent to go in search of the truth.

It will wrench her heart to let him go. The seas took one man from her already; will they take this one as well, this youth she remembers as a babe at her breast? But release him she will, because perhaps he will find what she cannot: an escape from this trap, for himself, for her, for them all.

He will board the ship and go to Pylos, to Sparta, and in the halls of a king he will indeed hear the tale. Full of joy, he will set sail for home—but on the beaches of Ithaka, he will find a different welcome.

Antinoös, Ktesippos, Elatos, and others besides. Armed and armored, prepared not for war, but for murder. There on the beaches they will cut her son down, and his blood will flower like anemones in the sand.

When the news reaches her, it will break her heart. She will fling herself from the walls of Ithaka, and her sole victory will be that none among her suitors will ever claim her.

She wants to weep, seeing what she has woven. The threads fight her, their orderly arrangement belying their potential for chaos. Each thread is a life, and each life is a thousand thousand choices; she is not goddess enough to control them. Only a woman, a mortal woman, with a trace of the divine in her veins. And a trace is not enough.

It has become far too familiar, this unweaving. Forward and

back make little difference to the speed and surety of her hands. Melantho gathers up the loose thread silently, winds it back onto the shuttle, but her mistress does not miss the sullen look in the girl's eyes. This is one who has made her life pleasant by giving herself to the men. She does not like being a maidservant, even to a queen.

A queen who can trace her ancestry back through her grandmother's grandmother to the three daughters of Necessity. From them she inherits this fragment of their gift, to spin thread and link it to men, to weave the shape of their fates on her loom. If she continues her efforts….

But she has no chance to try again. When she goes to that high chamber the next morning, Leodes is there, and the frame is bare of threads. He knows what she has been doing; they all know, for Melantho has told them. Leodes has always been more tolerable than the others, for he is their priest, and alone among them he respects the obligations of a guest. He chides her now for her dishonesty, though, for lying to them all this time about the progress of her weaving. There will be no more thread for her, no days and nights spent safe in this room, trying to weave a path away from danger.

He leaves her there with the empty frame and empty hands. She is not without choices: she has woven a hundred of them, a thousand, a new one every day. But every one ends in disaster. She will not choose disaster.

In fury she takes up her scissors. There are no threads here for her to cut; she sets the blades instead to her hair. When she wed she cut a single lock in sacrifice; now she cuts them all. She kindles a fire in a bronze dish and gives her hair to the flames, an offering to the powers from whom she descends. If she cannot weave a good fate with her own hands, then she will pray for those powers to have pity upon her instead.

The flames rise high, dancing twisting flickering tongues, weaving about one another in ephemeral knots. In their light, she sees her answer, and she thrusts her hands into the fire.

When she withdraws them, threads of gold follow.

She casts them quickly into the air, the steady lines of the warp, the glowing bundle of the weft. There, without loom, without doubt, she begins to weave the fate of one man.

He is on the island of Kalypso, prisoner and guest. The nymph sings as she walks to and fro across her loom, weaving with a shuttle of gold. But Kalypso is no kin to the Fates. Her pattern will falter, give way to a power stronger than her own.

The gods themselves will order his release. One will try to drown him at sea, but he will come safe to the island of the Phaiakians. There he will find hospitality and tales of the war in years past, and one—the tale of his most clever stratagem—will provoke him to admit his true name.

He will tell them his tale, the long years since that war, and out of respect they will aid him in his final journey. In the house of the swineherd Eumaios his son will find him: Telemachos, evading the trap Antinoös has laid. Together they will devise a new strategem. The king will return to his palace as a beggar, to be ridiculed and mocked by the men who have impoverished his house for so long.

And she...

She will put a challenge before her suitors, to string and shoot her husband's bow. One after another they will try and fail, until the filthy old beggar does what they cannot. And then he will turn his bow upon them, until every man among them lies dead.

Odysseus, King of Ithaka, will come home at last.

The tapestry hangs in the air before her, a perfect creation, glowing with fire and hope.

In the darkness beyond, her half-blinded eyes discern a silhouette. A woman, helmed and regal, who studies her work with a critical eye.

Her own gaze follows, and she sees the flaw. The error which, perhaps, underlay all others, turning her every bid for victory into failure. And she knows how it must be mended.

It is not easy to cast the final row. To cloud her own mind, robbing herself of this memory, the knowledge that she has woven Odysseus' fate and through him, the fate of them all. But she must. If she knows what is to come, she will ruin it; she will betray the truth through a careless word or a too-cautious act. There is a reason this gift is a thing of gods and not mortals.

The thread settles into place, binding her own fate. She will see her husband and not know him; recognition will not come until he proves himself to her again.

Her weaving is done. She kneels before the grey-eyed goddess and bows her head, accepting the ignorance that wisdom bestows. The brilliant light of her creation flares and then fades away.

Her maids find her collapsed on the floor and hurry her off to bed. These are the ones whose threads will continue; they have kept faith with their queen, and so they will not be hanged with treacherous Melantho and her sisters. But all of that lies in a future they have not seen. Neither maid nor mistress knows what she has done.

She sleeps a day and a night, and when she rises, her hair is as long as it ever was. She goes about her duties in a daze, which her maids attribute to the absence of her son. Their reasoning is borne out when Telemachos returns, for then it seems that she wakes at last from her dream.

She goes to the head of the hall, looking out over her suitors, the men who have clamored for her hand, believing her to be the means by which they will shape their own fates.

The old beggar stands disregarded at the back of the hall. In this moment, every eye is upon her.

Penelope holds the mighty bow in her hand and speaks for all to hear. "My husband will be the man who can string the bow of Odysseus, and fire an arrow through twelve axe-heads. Thus the Fates have decreed, and on my word, it shall be so."

Your Body, My Prison, My Forge

LUNGS. STOMACH. BONES. Heart. I will use every piece of you I can in order to craft what I require. You will not enjoy the process, I think…but you should have thought of that before you swallowed me whole.

For one who has sired so many, I suspect you know little of what happens after your part is done. Women who are bearing often crave odd foods, as if something inside them needs what is in those things. Whether you like it or not, *you* are now bearing—after a fashion—and I need copper. Tin. Count yourself lucky that the arsenical variety of bronze will not serve my purpose. You eat the metals, forcing them into your mouth and down your throat, and deep inside your body I receive them. This kind of working is unfamiliar to me, though I know the principles; I will waste far too much in mistakes. You may expect to eat more before I am done.

First the alloying, testing different proportions, seeking the ones best-suited to my needs. When I think I have them right, I carve clay from your muscles and shape a mold. I heat my alloy in the fires of your stomach—your recent meals have not agreed with you—then pour the molten bronze in through the opening of the sprue. Waiting for it to cool seems to last forever; I must fight the urge to strike the clay open too soon. But my patience does me no good: the object inside is misshapen anyway, marred by voids in some places, lumps in others where it spilled beyond the confines of the mold. I throw the failure back into your stomach. Mistakes are to be expected, and they do not bother me. I will be trapped here a long time; I need something with which to occupy myself.

Something besides the thing you feared, the thing that made you swallow me alive.

I shape mold after mold, not holding back when you twist in pain at me digging into your muscles again. My tools are of bone, stolen from here and there around your body. I use your lungs as my bellows, your heart as the engine for my hammer. Too many blows make the bronze too brittle; working it hot does not help, nor does quenching it in your blood, and the latter makes you convulse in agony. By slow trial and error I learn to anneal the metal, heating it and then cooling it slowly. I do that not to spare you, but to make my crafting the best it can be.

Our daughter must have the best.

Do I spend too long at my forge, too many hours heating and cooling and hammering and pouring? At first I do not think so. When I am upstairs in your head, my gaze inevitably strays toward your eyes, just as your eyes themselves stray. Of all the gods, you are the most fickle: after me there is another wife, then another after her, then another still. Had you not swallowed me, I doubt I would be at your side today. I am neither forgiving enough to endure your infidelities, nor proud enough to insist on staying regardless.

It is pride and lack of forgiveness both that send me back to my forge, to the metal I slowly bend to my will. The spearhead is my first success, and if I prick you a few too many times to test the sharpness of its point, that is only fair. Years have gone by since you swallowed me. If only you had been imprisoned along with your siblings; then you might understand the frustration of what you have done to me.

The spearhead. Then the breastplate, marked with chalky bone so I know where to hammer in the contours. Then the greaves, easy by comparison. I roll the edges so they will lie comfortably against the leg, and then I take a little while to cast decorations for those and the breastplate alike.

There was a time I would not have bothered with that. Such niceties delay me starting on the helmet, and therefore delay the completion of my task. But now…now I find myself reluctant to finish too soon.

Somehow, like the slow, creeping growth of a vine, I have become fond.

Not of this prison—never that. But as the days dwindle, I find myself regretting my earlier haste. I spend more time in your head, and now it is not the view from your eyes that demands my attention. I find myself thinking that I could have taken more rest away from the forge, broken up those long hours of work with idleness. Even play. Instead I let my anger drive me, and it blinded me to what was slipping away. Now the work is nearly done, and once it is…I will be truly alone.

So be it. I will miss her—I will mourn the hours that could have been—but I will not trap her in here with me. Like the fires of my forge, my anger has burned out; this is no longer about striking back against you. It is about what our daughter deserves.

When the helmet is ready at last, I arm and armor my beautiful child, taller than I am, but her eyes the same grey as mine. And as I do, I tell her the story one final time: how her great-grandparents spoke a prophecy that I would bear children wiser than you. How you tricked me into becoming a fly and swallowed me, hoping to prevent that fate—proof enough of how little wisdom *you* have. But I already carried your child; here inside you I gave birth to her. And here inside you I forged her weapons and armor. At first so that she might be my champion in the world, but now…now it is so that she might be arrayed in the glory she deserves.

She kisses me, thanks me, bids me farewell. We both know I must remain behind. The prophecy spoke also of a son, and if I give you reason to fear a second child, you will not stop at merely imprisoning me. Instead I will stay in your head as your cunning, your *metis*. And I will try not to resent it when people credit you with the ideas I create.

I take my hammer and strike it against the curve of your skull, this chamber that has been my daughter's home as she grew from babe to woman. Again and again I strike, my rhythm steady and strong from years of forging.

Until a blow answers me from without, and cracks your skull open.

After so much time inside, I find the light blinding. But not nearly as radiant as my precious Athene, crowned with the helm I made for her, bearing my spear in hand, as she steps from your head into the world.

For the Fairest

FOR THE FAIREST, the inscription read. It spread discord aplenty, as intended. The goddesses squabbled and shrieked, and if beauty were judged to be internal as well as external, none of them were terribly pretty in that moment. The gods knew better than to get directly involved. They passed that responsibility to a mortal, and washed their hands of the whole affair.

The three front-runners, meanwhile, offered the best bribes they could think up: wisdom, power, love. Any normal man would have given his left arm for any one of the three.

But the judge was not a normal man, and the squabbling goddesses—as well as the one who had thrown the apple in the first place—failed to take into account the truly phenomenal size of his ego.

For the fairest, the inscription read. The prince of Troy, handsome even in his rustic shepherd's garb, buffed the apple's golden surface, nodded in approval at his reflection, and smiled at the goddesses as he walked away.

The Wives of Paris

THEY OFFERED HIM a beautiful woman, power over men, victory in war.

So of course he chose the beautiful woman. He was a young man, after all. Power would come—don't forget, he was the son of a king—and victory was guaranteed, because all young men are invincible…but a woman's soft thighs are another matter. To a teenager, that is the fruit of Tantalus: only divine intervention can bring it within reach.

Aphrodite cleared up his acne, taught him how to flirt, and sent him off to Sparta. And the rest is well-known myth.

Never mind Oenone. (No one ever does.) Menelaus, sure, people remember him; how many guys start a war over a simple case of adultery? Nobody remembers the nymph Paris abandoned. Even though she did the Morgan le Fay thing, and sent her son—Paris' son—to try and betray Troy to the Greeks. Even though she did the Hallgerðr thing, and refused Paris the assistance that might have saved his life. Even though she did the thing done by women in tales the world over, and committed suicide after he was dead.

Oenone, Οἰνώνη, nymph of wine. Maybe she was drunk when she met Paris. She wouldn't be the first woman to make that mistake, seeing a young man, *knowing* he's going to break her heart, and giving it to him anyway. Sure, she had more than just instinct to warn her; she had *prophecy*. But who ever pays attention to that?

❧

Say Paris was different. Still seventeen years old, still exiled from Troy to herd sheep on Mount Ida, but with more on his mind than just sex. After all, he's married to a nymph, and we all know what *they're* like, the little tarts. He's already getting enough action.

A beautiful woman, power over men, victory in war. He's never seen war, but power sounds nice. More interesting than this hillside, anyway. Especially when Hera dangles the extra incentive of gold, jewels, riches beyond his (rather limited) imagination. Oenone never seems to care that she's married beneath herself, that he's a sheepherder and she's an immortal nymph, but it bugs him.

So he tells Aphrodite her ass is too fat for his taste, and hands the golden apple to Hera. Hey presto, power.

It takes a little longer than that, of course. She isn't a genie, to conjure up a kingdom for Paris out of thin air, and bumping off his dad (not to mention his forty-nine brothers) to make him King of Troy seems rather in poor taste. But marriage, that's a respectable road to both power and riches.

Enter Lamia. (Hera can see the future, too. Leave any woman unattended for long enough, and Zeus will try to sleep with her; it seems kinder to make sure Lamia is attended than to get vengeance later by making her eat her own children.) She's a queen of Libya, and as she hasn't yet ripped out her own eyes over the kids-for-dinner thing, she's passably pretty. No Helen, but then again who is, and since Paris has never laid eyes on Helen, it doesn't much matter. This is a political match anyway, made for the purpose of world domination.

She's always wanted to take over Egypt. Not with an army; armies are unsubtle things, and Lamia has a serpent's subtlety. Instead she and her new husband offer a trade-pact here, a treaty there, a marriage of some Egyptian daughter to a Libyan son. (Paris acknowledges the boy as his own, and that's enough for political purposes, even though the kid's skin is black as coal.) Pretty soon various Greek cities are client-states to the North

African empire. Their caravans and ships venture from the Pillars of Hercules to the far reaches of the East, bringing back spices and emeralds and letters of friendship from foreign potentates.

Nobody besieges the gates of Troy. Why should they? It's a backwater, a forgotten little city, neglected by the great power that now rules half the known world and has alliances with the other half. Paris hasn't forgotten that his father dumped him on Mount Ida to herd sheep. Old Priam lives long enough to see his kingdom wither, starved for trade, its young people migrating to greener pastures. Twenty-three of Paris' brothers end up working for the Libyan court, in one minor clerical position or another. Not Hector, of course; it's beneath a crown prince's dignity. He puts together a force of warriors instead, intending to attack whatever target presents itself. They never make it out the door: Priam keels over of a very convenient heart attack, so everything stops for the funeral games, and while that's going on Hector discovers Troy's in debt up to its eyeballs. Faced with a choice between selling himself in marriage to some foreign princess, and watching what remains of his kingdom be carved up among its neighbors, he falls on his sword.

Paris never hears about any of this. Lamia sees to it that his flunkies don't trouble him with such insignificant trifles.

Oenone's heart is broken, of course. Paris didn't abandon her on Mount Ida; he and Lamia agreed from the start that there's no reason to expect marital fidelity, so long as there are enough acknowledged children to marry off for alliances. But Oenone pines for their days of bucolic peace; at this remove, it's easy to forget the annoyance and toil that caring for sheep actually requires. She preferred the sheepherder to the king, anyway. She feels like she doesn't even know Paris anymore.

She goes to tell him this, and he stares blankly at her, like she's speaking—well, not Greek. Russian, maybe. Weeping, Oenone asks if he knows *her* anymore.

A flunky, ushering the devastated nymph out the door, explains that they don't trouble the king with such insignificant trifles as her name.

☙❧

So power corrupts—but we knew that already. And thinking with the downstairs brain never ends well. What's behind door number three?

Up the aggression a bit, and you've got a Paris who dreams of glory on the battlefield. The daughter of Zeus is more cunning than her sisters, or whatever you call the wife of the guy whose head you sprang out of, and the chick born from the sea foam created by the genitals of a dead ur-god. (No doubt the Germans can build nouns for these things.) She doesn't dangle breasts or gold. She merely looks at him, and *looks* at him, until he squirms and reddens and decides he's got to prove something to the grey-eyed bitch. Victory in war, please, and you other two can shove off.

Athena makes him earn it—which means he has to learn something other than sheep—which means he needs a teacher. All the fashionable heroes go to Chiron, but she's bored with the centaur's style, and decides to try something new. She sends him to Penthesilea.

The Queen of the Amazons gives Paris plenty of reason to regret his choice. Her followers are less than pleased with having to train a man; they threaten to cut off his balls several times a week. (The threats are that often, not the cutting. Unlike Prometheus' liver, his balls would *not* grow back.) And the training itself is boot camp from hell, for a fellow whose most vigorous exercise until now has been sporting with a nymph. But Penthesilea is nothing if not determined, and after a while they both start to enjoy it, the discipline and the shouting matches and eventually the sex, which is nothing like it was with gentle Oenone.

Hercules. Theseus. Achilles….and Paris. Menelaus wouldn't be able to kick *this* kid's ass, not once Penthesilea is done with him. The Amazons abandon her, muttering in disgust about that prick corrupting their queen, but the two of them hardly care. Together Paris and his warrior-wife rampage around the Mediterranean, collecting an army of rabid followers and laying waste every kingdom and city-state you care to name, before returning to Troy in triumph. There Paris "suggests" to his aged father and forty-nine brothers that maybe it's time for a fresh rump on the throne. They're smart enough not to argue.

And when the debts of his rampage come due, nobody breaks a sweat. So what if every kingdom and city-state in the Mediterranean wants a piece of Troy's hide? Their king's got Athena on his side. She won't let him lose.

Not in war, anyway. But she promised him victory, not wisdom, and nobody planned for Oenone. Nor for the Amazons, who haven't forgotten that their queen waltzed off with some dick-swinging jerk. Jilted nymph plus psychotic warriors equals a plan that, while not as iconic as a giant wooden horse with Greeks inside, gets the job done.

One hundred harlots enter the city of Troy. Ninety-nine disperse through the soldiers' quarters, gritting their teeth into something like a smile. The hundredth makes her way up to the palace, where she pours poisoned wine down the throats of her erstwhile husband and the bitch he ran off with.

It doesn't take ten years. It doesn't even take ten hours. Half the soldiery is dead by morning, and the gates are jammed open; every Trojan with common sense grabs their portable wealth and flees. What's left descends into chaos and looting, and when the armies finally show up, they burn what little remains.

Stop me if you've heard this one before. There's a kid, and you just *know* he's going to be trouble, so you decide to prevent it by offing him. Only you're too squeamish to actually do the deed, so instead you handle it in a roundabout way—abandoning him on a mountainside, say, where you can be deceived about the attempt's success.

It didn't work for the parents of Oedipus; it didn't work for the uncle of Romulus and Remus—hell, it didn't work for Snow White's step-mother—but why mess with tradition? Off to the mountainside with little baby Paris. As proof of his death, the herdsman presents a dog's tongue. And Priam and Hecuba sleep soundly, knowing they sent their son off to be murdered…but at least he won't be the ruin of his homeland, as the prophets had foretold.

Except he will, of course, because Fate's a bitch—three of them—and mountainsides never work like they're supposed to. You can't blame Helen: her face may have launched a thousand ships, but Paris is the one who brought them to Troy. He was always going to bring destruction. Athena and Hera couldn't change that. No woman, mortal or divine, could.

Nor even poor, forgotten Oenone. Paris' first wife, who knew he was going to break her heart, and gave it to him anyway. Get rid of the golden, discord-causing apple; get rid of the three goddesses who have nothing better to do with their time than squabble about who's the prettiest. Leave him there on Mount Ida, a simple shepherd with his nymphly wife.

He'll *still* find a way to bring it down.

But maybe there's happiness in that simplicity, before it falls apart. No politics; no bloodshed; no marriages broken by an adulterous spouse.

And no epic poetry, spanning the gulf of ages, singing of glorious tragedy.

Oenone would not complain.

WEST ASIAN

The Me of Perfect Sight

THE HALL OF the Abzu-temple was impossibly vast, and impossibly full. On shelves to either side, on tables down the center, stood the holy *me*: the decrees of Anu, the supreme god of the land between the rivers, which made all things of the world come into being.

Enki, god of the waters, god of the earth, walked the length of the hall. Past the *me* of the exalted and enduring crown; past the *me* of the destruction of cities; past the *me* of the craft of the leatherworker. The *me* of lamentation; the *me* of rejoicing of the heart; the *me* of holy purification—to all of them he paid no heed, until he came to the end of the hall, and the farthest corner of the highest shelf.

Enki, god of mischief, god of knowledge, reached out his hand and took up the *me* of perfect sight.

Time and space unfolded for him like the petals of a lotus. He looked at the *me* of the flood, and he saw the Tigris and Euphrates, the Nile, the Yellow River, the Mississippi. He saw the heroes of the great flooding of the earth: Atrahasis, Noah, Dà Yŭ, Bergelmir, Cessair, Manuśraddhādeva, Deucalion and Pyrrha.

He looked at the *me* of kingship, and he saw a rex, a raja, an oba, a tsar. He saw kindly kings and cruel kings, wise kings and foolhardy kings, kings beheaded by their subjects, kings overthrown and their thrones left empty. He saw Arthur and the fall of Camelot, Jimmu and a line that lasted for thousands of years.

He looked at the *me* of descent into the underworld, and he saw a crucifix, a ball of heavy rubber, a pomegranate seed. He looked at the *me* of ascent from the underworld, and he saw a divine corpse taken from a hook; he saw a man turning to look back too soon. He saw the holy form of that *me* dropped to the floor of a cave in horror at the sight of putrefaction—and because of that loss, ages later, the light of the frozen north would stay in the land of Hel.

Enki, god of creation, god of crafts, looked at the *me* of family.

He saw his daughter Inanna; he saw his granddaughter Inanna. He saw her come to his Abzu-temple. He looked at the *me* of inebriation and saw Inanna cunningly plying him with beer; he saw himself drunkenly pledging to her all the *me* within this hall, hers to claim and use as she willed. He looked at the *me* of the *sukkal* and saw himself sending that lieutenant to take back what he had promised to Inanna; he saw Inanna's *sukkal* raise her sword in response and defeat the monsters he sent against her. He looked at all the *me* that filled his hall and saw them gone, taken away to be placed in the great city of Uruk, the holy city of Inanna.

Fury rose in his heart. Was he some weak-willed fool, to be robbed of his treasures so easily? Was he to be the laughingstock of the world, deceived by his own kin? Having seen the trap laid for his feet, how could he fail to avoid it now?

He gazed the length of the hall, taking in all the holy *me*, all the things made by Anu for the world. Like a mosaic, the single pieces formed a larger whole—and in the image they formed, he saw civilization rise in Uruk. Then fall, then rise again, countless times through the ages, in countless places between the rivers and in the lands beyond them.

Enki looked at the *me* of perfect sight.

He called to his *sukkal*, ordering that butter cakes and cold water be given to Inanna when she came, ordering that his bronze vessels be filled with beer—strong beer, lakes and oceans of it, enough to render even a god drunk.

Then he took the *me* of perfect sight and smashed it against the floor.

In later ages, shards of that shattered decree would find their way to other lands. They would pierce the eyes and hearts of gods and spirits and mortals, granting slivers of the power that had once been. But the *me* of perfect sight was broken; the visions it had granted slipped from his mind. Never again would anyone hold it in their hand and see with flawless clarity all that would come to pass.

Enki, god of wisdom, left the hall of his Abzu-temple, and went to bid Inanna welcome.

The Gospel of Nachash

1.

IN THE BEGINNING God made the world, and on the sixth day he made creatures in his image. Male and female he created them, and they were the bekhorim, to whom God gave dominion over every herb bearing seed, and every tree bearing fruit, to be in their care. Mankind he formed from dust, but the bekhorim were made from air, and their spirits were more subtle than that of man.

Then the LORD planted a garden eastward in Eden; and there he put the man he had formed, and the bekhorim tended the garden, for they had dominion over all growing things. And he gave to each of them a duty, saying, each tree in the garden you shall tend, and each of you shall have a tree, which shall be as meat for mankind, and for the beasts of the field. But of the tree of knowledge of good and evil they shall not eat.

Among the bekhorim there was one called Nachash, and to him it was given to tend the tree of knowledge of good and evil. And Nachash was saddened, for all his kindred had purpose, but he had none, for man and woman ate of every tree in the garden save his, and he labored without purpose.

He went therefore to the woman, who was called Chava, and said unto her, Yea, hath God said, Ye shall not eat of every tree of the garden?

And the woman said unto Nachash, We may eat of the fruit of the trees of the garden: but of the fruit of the tree which is in the midst of the garden, God hath said, Ye shall not eat of it, neither shall ye touch it, lest ye die.

But the tree was the tree of knowledge of good and evil, and Nachash knew of no death in it. And for what purpose did it bear fruit, if not to be eaten? Therefore he said to the woman, Ye shall not surely die, for in the day ye eat thereof, then your eyes shall be opened, and ye shall be as gods, knowing good and evil.

And when the woman saw that the tree was good for food, and that it was pleasant to the eyes, and a tree to be desired to make one wise, she took of the fruit thereof, and did eat, and gave also unto her husband with her; and he did eat.

And the LORD God was wroth with them, and expelled them from the garden. And the bekhorim he expelled likewise, for the sin of Nachash, who had beguiled the woman into eating. Their forms he altered in divers ways; but Nachash he cast down upon his belly, to crawl in the dust from which man had come. He placed at the east of the garden of Eden Cherubim, and a flaming sword which turned every way, to keep the way of the tree of life.

2.

Thus were the bekhorim made wanderers in the lands outside of Eden, which were as a wilderness, full of thistles and thorns. For the LORD had cursed the ground, that Adam might labor with much toil to bring forth food from it, and for the bekhorim it was likewise cursed; that which was their dominion was now fallen into ruin. And the bekhorim lamented, saying, we are condemned; for the sin of Nachash we are condemned.

But he had sinned unknowing, for Nachash had not eaten of the fruit of the tree. Of good and evil the bekhorim were ignorant.

Now it came to pass that many among them sickened and became weak. In the Garden there had been neither sickness nor death, nor any ill thing, but in the wilderness beyond there was much confusion, for no creature yet had knowledge of death. And the LORD God went to the tree of life and took from it a branch; and from that branch he formed a creature, shaped like unto the bekhorim, and breathed life into her, saying, this is my daughter, for she is created from me. And she was called Anaph, because she was born from the tree of life.

The bekhorim were then living in the lands west of Eden. Nachash lived not among them, but skulked and crawled at the edges of their camps, and whenever one saw him, that one threw a stone, to drive him forth. Yet one day he came within their camp and said to them, Send me not away, for I have had a vision, which comes from the LORD God. He hath shown me a wind out of the east, where Eden lies; and this wind bringeth a great mystery, which is the mystery of life and death. Follow me into the east, that we may greet this wind, and know the will of God.

But the people jeered and did not believe. They said, Why should the LORD show this vision to thee, for whose transgression we are all condemned? And in their hearts they were afraid, that if they approached the garden they would be struck down, by the angels who kept the way of the tree of life.

Therefore Nachash went alone, journeying forty days and nights through the wilderness, until he faltered with weakness and thirst. He said, Though I can go no further, my faith endures; I will lie here in the dust, and await the coming of that which is promised. And in that moment he felt wind upon his face.

The wind was the coming of Anaph, who came as a storm and a whirlwind, driving all the dust before her. Yet when she laid her hand upon his face, her touch was gentle, despite that there was strength in it; and with her touch Nachash was revived, and opened his eyes. Before him he saw a glory so terrible he hid his face, saying, You are an angel of the LORD, and I am not worthy to look upon your face.

Look, said Anaph, and Nachash looked; and now she was as any bekhira, but he did not forget the glory he had seen. She said unto him, I am the wind that was promised, and I bring the mystery of life and death, which few will understand. Because thou alone hast sought me, I will make of thee my first disciple, and to thee shall be given to understand more than all the others.

Nachash bowed his head and said, You honor me more than I deserve.

No honor, said Anaph, but a terrible burden, for the mystery of life and death is both cruel and kind. Thou wilt grieve for thy decision to seek me here, and be despised for its consequence. Yet I tell thee truly, all of this must come to pass, for it is the will of my Father the LORD God.

And Nachash did not understand, but bowed his head again, and accepted the burden Anaph laid upon him, which in later times brought much grief to his people.

3.

Westward she went with Nachash, him upon his belly in the dust behind her, until she came to a camp of the bekhorim. And when they saw her they were much surprised, for their kind were few in number, though not so few as man; strangers had they none. Yet they welcomed her in; but when they saw Nachash in the dust at her heels they halted, saying, Here is one who is not welcome. For his wrongdoing we were expelled, though we are guiltless of his crime.

Guiltless you are not, said Anaph, for all your kind are kindred, and what tainteth the one tainteth the many. Yet I say to you, be not wroth with him; all this was foreseen by the LORD God, from whom nothing is concealed, and nothing may happen without He permits it. You must allow him into your camps, for none should ever be exiled from among yourselves, however great his crime.

And they said unto her, Who are you to know these things, that are a stranger to us?

She answered them, A miracle hath come to pass with Chava and Adam. On the day I was created, so too was life created within Chava's womb; on the day I set forth on my journey, so too did her travails begin, the great pain which the LORD promised her. And when Nachash opened his eyes and beheld me, yea, at that very moment, she put forth new life, which is a son, and he is named Qayin. For a branch hath come forth from the tree of life, and the spirit of the LORD hath gone into it, and I am that branch, sent unto you.

But many among them believed not, for they did not understand the mystery she had imparted regarding Chava and her son. Neither did they understand Anaph herself, for they believed the LORD had turned his back upon them, condemning them to sickness and suffering.

She went therefore among them and found one, a mighty bekhor, whose body was grown weak, so that he could no longer lift himself from where he lay. And she stretched forth her hand, and when she touched him, strength grew once more within him. Thereupon he leapt up as if newly created. Then he knelt at the feet of the daughter of God and said, I know not who you are, but you have given me back my strength; for that I will follow you to the ends of the earth.

She said unto him, Follow me and thou shalt bear that which thou understandest not, for this is the will of the LORD, that the bekhorim, his first-born, should bear to mankind this mystery, which is for them. And he was called Koach, and became her second disciple.

She went then among the camps of the bekhorim, and wherever she found sickness, she had but to lay her hand upon the one who sickened, and that one became well. She performed great miracles in this manner, and some who witnessed her miracles followed her, even as Nachash followed her. They complained greatly of this, asking why he should go before them, who was the source of all their guilt. But Anaph told them he must be at her heels, for she had laid a burden upon him, and he must stay with her until he had delivered it unto its fruition.

4.

These were the disciples of Anaph: Koach, and Gidul, and Yofi, and Savlan; Ometz, and Yedida, and Tikvah, and Machshava. And Nachash was the ninth.

To these nine she taught many things, which were hints of the LORD's plan for the bekhorim. She therefore took them apart, and sat with them upon a hill, and spoke, saying,

You are the first-born creations of the LORD, the elder brothers and sisters of mankind. And it is right for the elder to teach to the younger, knowing things of the world which the younger hath not learned. For this you shall be rewarded.

I bring to you the mystery of life and death, which is to govern the world now the gate of Eden hath been barred. On this day Chava hath brought forth a second son, who is called Hevel, and in this manner shall all of mankind be propagated: in woman's desire for her husband shall the seed be planted, and in pain for their sins shall she bring it forth. And their days upon the earth shall not be without number; in time their strength shall wane, and when that hour comes their souls shall depart their bodies, going to their heavenly Father to be judged. But of that mystery none among the bekhorim may speak, nay, not even myself; for that is reserved to mankind alone.

Through me do they gain this gift of life, but you must bear it to them. As once you tended the trees in the garden, now shall you inhabit the wilderness without; to you the LORD gave dominion over every herb bearing seed, and every tree bearing fruit, to be in your care. You shall be of the trees, and of the waters, and of the airy winds, and of all things giving life. For you there shall be no weakness, nor any departure; you shall neither eat nor drink, save by your own desire, and the toil of mankind is not for you. Eternal shall your lives be, and this is the gift of the LORD to his first-born creations.

So taught Anaph, and the disciples marveled at her words.

Then she laid the commandments of God upon them, saying, Remember always the day of your birth, which was the sixth day of creation; and celebrate it with your actions. Fear the name of the LORD, for it is fitting that the eldest show respect by their fear. Give not your own names to those who might abuse them; names are holy things, and in them is power. Break not your oaths to any creature, for as light and all things came into being upon the word of the LORD, so too do your words call forth the thing which you swear; to render them false is to destroy that which you have created, which is an abomination.

These were the teachings of Anaph to her eight disciples, and to Nachash, who was the ninth, and first among them all.

5.

After Anaph had wrought many miracles among the bekhorim, and taught to them their holy covenant, she drew apart for a time. And Nachash stayed by her side, for he had been with her since she opened his eyes in the wilderness, and he bore great love for her. Recognizing this, Anaph said unto him, It is not good that thou holdest me thus in thy heart, for it will only make heavier the burden thou bearest. But Nachash said, It is only through my love that I was saved; though I am not yet redeemed, for I still go upon my belly in the dust. I will obey any commandment of yours, save that which commands me not to love.

Then she gathered together her disciples and once more imparted to them the will of God, saying, Chava hath borne two sons unto Adam, who are Qayin and Hevel; she will in time bear more, and daughters besides. But it is not fitting for a man to marry his sister, nor for a woman to lie with her brother; it is an abomination. How then are the generations of mankind to continue? I say to you, this is the gift the bekhorim shall bear to them, taken from the hand of the LORD. Two of you must go forth now to the place where Chava and Adam dwell, and give yourselves as wives to their sons. And before you depart I shall baptize you, and wash from you the gifts given to the bekhorim, that you may receive the gifts of mankind; human you will be, and bear sons and daughters to the sons and daughters of Adam.

When the disciples heard this, they were much disturbed. They went apart from Anaph to consider her words in the stillness of their hearts. But when the bekhorim heard what had passed among them, many were wroth, and the angry ones said,

We are the eldest children of the LORD, and favored in his eyes: for us there is no toil or sweat, no sickness and no death. Why should we abandon these gifts to become less than we are? For Anaph said also that others must go: until the numbers of Adam's seed grew so many that one might not be close cousin to all the rest, they must take their husbands and their wives from among the bekhorim, who thereafter would be human.

And even those who heeded Anaph yet questioned, asking, Is it not fitting that the seed of Adam should give something to us in return? This sacrifice is asked of us alone, whose numbers are few and unchanging; why should we not have compensation out of the multitudes of his children, to console us for those we have lost?

She answered them, saying, Consolation shall be yours, for when it is needed, you shall bear children, and not with the pains of Chava. As you bring life to mankind, so must they bring it to you; they shall be your midwives when that time comes, that your numbers may be restored. And this reassured many, but not all.

Her disciples then came to her again, and Anaph asked them for their answer. And Ometz stepped forward and said, I will be wife to Qayin, and Yedida followed her, saying, I will be wife to Hevel. To them Anaph said, Sorrows you both shall know, for hard is the way for those who first break the path; but you shall be rewarded for your choice.

Then she took them to the banks of the river, and there she washed from them the guilt of Nachash, so they were bekhorot no more, but as women. But she clothed them in green, in remembrance of their former natures, and thus they went forth to the place where Adam and Chava dwelt, and there gave themselves as wives to Qayin and Hevel. And Anaph said, Keep the memory of this act, as your tribute to Heaven, and to the Father who gave you life; that in future times others may go unto mankind and cleave to them as wives. But let mankind treasure that which hath been given to them, and mistreat it not, lest they lose that which they have received.

6.

And to the six of her disciples that remained, and to also Nachash, Anaph said, The final mystery is soon to come, which shall seal your covenant with the LORD. Truly I say to you, though you understand it not, this is the fruition of all that my Father hath willed for you; for I am born of the tree of life, and this is the fruit I give unto you. Take, eat; by this are you washed clean of the guilt of Nachash, and made holy again in the eyes of the LORD.

And the disciples did not understand. But Anaph drew apart with Nachash, and said to him in secret, This is the burden laid upon thee, that thou must understand more than all the rest. Unto Qayin thou must go, and counsel him; for the time hath come for the sons of Chava to make an offering unto the LORD. And he is a tiller of the ground, as his brother is a keeper of sheep, and from this will each make his offering: but unto Qayin thou shalt go, and tell him there is a fruit he must offer to the LORD.

But Nachash, fearing, said unto her, I cannot tell him of this offering, for in the silence of my heart a voice speaks, warning me that great grief will come of it.

Anaph said, And so it will. For it shall be as I warned thee: that thy greater understanding would be a burden, and thou wouldst be despised for it. Yet this is the mystery I bring to thee, that without death there cannot be life: whereas in the garden all was perfection, and neither life nor death were needed, here in the wilderness there must be both; and so I bring them. Through me did Chava bear her first son, and through me shall come also death, so that man's time upon this earth shall not be eternal, but only that of the bekhorim.

Then Nachash wept, for love abided in his heart, and so great was the pain that he thought this must be the death of which Anaph spoke. But death was not for the bekhorim. And he had promised her that he would obey any commandment, save the commandment not to love; and the bekhorim could not break their word, lest they commit an abomination.

7.

So he went forth, crawling upon his belly in the dust, until he came to the feet of Qayin. And to him he said, Go you into the wood, and you shall find there a tree, whose fruit is more pleasing than any that grow in this wilderness. Take with you your sickle, and reap from that tree, and offer its fruit unto the LORD. And Qayin thanked him and rewarded him, saying, For this gift I will give you a gift in return, that the first child my wife bears shall be yours to keep.

When Nachash returned all the disciples questioned him, asking, Where is Anaph, for we cannot find her. Then Nachash told them all she had said. Of the mystery they did not understand, but Koach saw the meaning of his words, and began to stamp upon his back, crying, Traitor. The others took up this cry, and threw stones at him, as they had in days past, saying, Traitor; thou hast betrayed our teacher, and because of thee she will die. And he lay beneath their feet, accepting their punishment.

At last Savlan halted them, saying, We must go find Qayin, and stop him, for he will slay our teacher.

In haste they went, and Nachash followed them, crawling in secret upon his belly, hidden by the grasses of the earth: but in haste also went Qayin, to the place where Nachash had told him the tree might be found. Together they came to that place, and there stood Anaph in the form of a tree; and Qayin took a jawbone, the sickle with which he reaped his crops, and swung it at the fruits of the tree; and they fell into his basket. But the blood of Anaph fell upon a stone, staining it red: which henceforth became anathema to the bekhorim, for it was the blood of their savior that made the stain within the stone. And a voice came out of the temple of Heaven, saying, It is done.

In that moment the tree withered and died. And the disciples, weeping, said, Where is the fruit that was promised to us? We have lost our teacher, the daughter of God; and in her place we have only desolation. And from the eyes of Nachash the tears fell unceasing.

8.

Then Qayin brought of the fruit of the tree an offering unto the LORD, and his brother Hevel brought of the firstlings of his flock and of the fat thereof. And the LORD had respect unto Hevel and to his offering: but unto Qayin and to his offering he had not respect. And Qayin was very wroth, and his countenance fell, for by his hand the savior of the bekhorim had died. But all this was intended by the LORD.

In the place of sacrifice, Nachash remained upon his belly in the grass, gazing upon the desolation of the tree. Then came to him one whose face he did not recognize, whose form was that of an angel, saying to him, For what cause do you weep?

Broken with grief, Nachash said, For the one who was my teacher and my love, who is now but dead wood before me; but truly for myself, who betrayed her, and who must now live with this pain until the day of judgment. For she brought death into the world, but it cometh not until its appointed hour, which lieth far off for me.

Unto him the other said, That need not be so.

Then he spoke divers things unto Nachash, of how the world might be changed; for if death were born untimely, then any creature might depart this earth and go to that which lay beyond. But Nachash said, Nothing lieth beyond, not for me, nor for any bekhor; for to mankind the LORD hath promised the paradise of the righteous, but to the bekhorim he hath promised nothing beyond this earth.

The other answered, You would end, and be no more; and be annihilated utterly. And to Nachash this seemed a thing to be desired, for it would bring an end to his grief.

He went therefore among his kindred, and again they drove him forth with stones. But many were angry, and to them he spoke, saying, Qayin hath killed our teacher; he hath slain the branch of the tree of life. To them we bring life, but to us they bring only death. And this perversion of the teachings the disciples did not hear, for they were occupied with their own grief.

To those who listened, Nachash promised a different covenant, saying, In this covenant shall the bekhorim be exalted, and not made servants to mankind; for we are first-born, and it is fitting that the eldest should have dominion over the youngest. From among them we will take our servants, and surrender none as their wives; to them we will give no gifts, but take that which is pleasing to us. And we shall have life eternal, a covenant sealed with blood.

He went therefore to Qayin, and to him he spoke, as once he had spoken to the woman Chava, but this time malice lived within his heart. He said, Why did the LORD have respect unto your brother and to his offering, and not unto you? Why should the younger be given the task of herding, that he might offer of the firstlings of his flock and of the fat thereof, and the blood which is pleasing to the LORD, while the elder toileth among the thorns and the thistles of the ground? For Nachash had hatred in his heart for Qayin, and this was the counsel given unto him by the one who found him in his desolation, that it should bring greater grief upon him.

Qayin went therefore to his brother Hevel, and walked in the field with him. And with the jawbone that cut down the branch of the tree of life he slew him, spilling the blood of his brother upon the ground, so that all the earth cried out. Then came the voice of the spirit of evil, saying, It is done; death hath entered the world untimely, and now man may die before his appointed hour. For Anaph had died at the time appointed by the LORD, but Hevel was the first to be murdered.

And the LORD said unto Qayin, Where is Hevel thy brother? And he said, I know not: am I my brother's keeper?

And he said, What hast thou done? the voice of thy brother's blood crieth unto me from the ground. And now art thou cursed from the earth, which hath opened her mouth to receive thy brother's blood from thy hand; when thou tillest the ground, it shall not henceforth yield unto thee her strength; a fugitive and a vagabond shalt thou be in the earth.

Thus was Qayin exiled from the presence of the LORD, with a mark upon him lest any should slay him; and this brought great joy unto Nachash, that he who spilled the blood of Anaph should suffer, and the gift of death should be denied him. But unto all the earth now that gift had been given: and so he went among the bekhorim who had heeded his words, saying, Remember this; slay their youths in the flower of their youth, before their appointed hour, in remembrance of the first murder. And this they did every seven years, on that night upon which Anaph was slain.

9.

But when half a year had passed after the murder of Hevel, a great wind sprang up in the lands about Eden, bearing a wondrous scent, as of blossoms and growing things; and all the wilderness came into bloom, though its glory was less than the garden of Eden. And the disciples went into the place of desolation, and there they found the tree that was dead now lived again, and upon its branches were a myriad of fruits. These they took and gave unto the people, and everyone who followed not the words of Nachash ate of them, and the fruit was the fruit of life. Then came Anaph among them once more, saying, This is my body, which hath been given for you.

At the sight of her all the people marveled, and her disciples fell at her feet. Six there were, for Ometz and Yedida had gone as wives to the sons of Adam, and Nachash came not among them now. And Anaph questioned them, saying, Where is my first disciple? and where is he upon whom I laid this burden, which was to betray me unto my death, that I might be born again? And the disciples said, Teacher, he is gone; he hath formed a new covenant, which is not a covenant with God.

And Anaph sorrowed, for her Father had foreseen all this, that Nachash would love her, and that his love would bring him to obey her; but upon her death it would lead him away once more, and into the path of evil. But of this Anaph herself had not known, and it grieved her.

Of the resurrection of Anaph Nachash had heard, for the

wind bore her touch to him. But he could not bear to look upon her again, with all the blood of his guilt upon her hands, and so he went once more into the wastelands about Eden, which were as wastelands no more, but blooming in the spring of her return. Unto the gates of Eden he went, and the Cherubim permitted him passage, and the flaming sword did not prevent him; unto the tree of knowledge of good and evil he went, which had once been in his care.

And of its fruit he ate, and understood what he had done. He cried out then, and Anaph heard him cry, and bowed her head in sorrow; for upon his understanding, he went without hesitation unto the tree of life, and from its branches he hanged himself. For the gift of the spirit of evil unto the bekhorim was the gift of death, which to them brings annihilation, and Nachash was no more.

10.

And in after times those who kept the holy covenant were called Seely, which means Blessed, but those who kept the covenant of Nachash were called Unseely, and they kept his pact with Hell. And unto both was given eternal life, but iron is anathema unto them, for its mark in the stone is the mark of the blood of Anaph, who was the tree of life, and slain by Qayin. All this was known beforehand to the LORD God, who permitted Nachash entrance into Eden, that one among the bekhorim might under-stand what had come to pass. But when the day of judgment comes, then all the bekhorim shall cease to be, for on that day their appointed hour will come, and for them there is only life eternal, but nothing to come after.

Salt Feels No Pain

SHE DID NOT mourn the cities in their fates, for they were full of wicked men. How often had she faced scorn and jeers in the courtyard by the well? How often had she feared for her safety as she walked the streets? Let them perish in fire and smoke. She would not weep for them.

But there was no salvation in leaving. The two cities were full of wicked men who would perish for their sins, but one such man was passing through the gates, departing, spared by the Lord for some perverse reason from the fate of his kind. Was she to follow him into the hills? Was she to continue her days serving a man who valued his guests above his daughters, who, instead of defending his door when the mob screamed outside, would offer his own children up to the wolves of the city, to be dishonored, debased, raped?

No.

She had endured it for years, but no more. She could not face more years of pain. She would not stay to see him drag his daughters into filth.

They had been warned not to look back. Lot obeyed. Why should he look back, when his daughters climbed the hills ahead of him, slender and young, tempting an old man's lascivious eyes?

But *she* looked back.

Her final thought was for her daughters, whom she could not protect from the foulness of their father. She felt pain for them. But then she turned, and saw Sodom and Gomorrah dying in fire—

and changed to salt—

and felt the pain no more.

At the Heart of Each Pearl
Lies a Grain of Sand

DURING THE REIGN of the famed Caliph Harun al-Rashid, the
world was a different and more wondrous place. Men daily went
to sea in search of profit or adventure; suffered the wreck of their
ships on account of monstrous beasts or terrible storms; washed
up on the shores of strange and mysterious islands; found there
riches beyond imagining, accommodating young women of great
beauty, or both; were rescued by helpful passing captains; and by
chance encountered men who could tell them the way back to
their far-distant homelands. Others came into possession of rings
and lamps and saddlebags which were the home of jinn, who
aided them against the schemes of their wicked and murderous
brothers; this commonly resulted in them living in palaces more
sumptuous than any sultan's treasury, by which means they took
the sultan's daughter to wife and his throne after he died.

But among all those astounding tales, there is perhaps none
more wondrous than this.

You may have heard one form of this tale, which begins with a
porter hired for an errand and a house inhabited by three beautiful
young women living in lonely splendor.

In the usual way of things, as those women were entertaining
their new friend the porter with a lavish meal, a knocking came at
their door. Soon they found themselves playing hostess to three
dervishes who all happened to be dispossessed princes afflicted by
the same wound, namely, blindness in their left eyes, though in all

cases the cause was different; and also of the disguised Caliph accompanied by his vizier, that pair being prone to wandering the streets of Baghdad disguised as common men. Together these assorted worthies sat down to a banquet of succulent chicken stuffed with raisins and rice, skewers of lamb marinated in fine spices, and sweets of pistachios and honey and figs. To slake their thirst they had wine (and sweetened rosewater for the pious Caliph), and incense perfumed the air.

But these three women had one request of their guests—porter, dervishes, and disguised vizier and Caliph alike—which was that they ask not about that which did not concern them. Of course the porter and the dervishes failed this test, for in those days hardly anyone could refrain from doing the single thing they had explicitly been told not to do, no matter how simple. Their questioning angered the ladies of the house, and for this they nearly lost their lives. But in the end they survived; so much for them.

The Caliph, however, held his tongue. He did this not out of virtue, but out of cunning: he had a plan, suggested to him by his vizier. The following day, having left that house, he sent his vizier to bring the three women to him.

They came into his halls of gold and veined marble, where pierced windows of sandalwood gently scented the breeze, and took their places behind a curtain to screen them from public view—but not before seeing the splendid Caliph. Gone was his simple turban of the night before, replaced by one so stiff with embroidered gold it might have deflected a sword. Then they knew their humble guest of the night before had been no such thing. And as the Caliph was no longer their guest, he wasted no time in asking each to tell her tale.

From the first he learned how she had suffered at the hands of her wicked and murderous sisters, whom a helpful jinniyah had subsequently transformed into a pair of dogs that she was required to whip each day, lest she too be condemned to life as a dog. As this was far from an unusual tale, the Caliph was not at all surprised, but rather summoned the jinniyah, whom he ordered to return the sisters to their natural shape. This the jinniyah did, and the first young woman forgave them, as people often did in those days.

From the second he learned how she had suffered at the hands of her jealous and controlling husband, who extracted from her an oath not to favor any man other than him; and when he believed she had broken her oath, he beat her so viciously she bore the scars to that very day. As this was far from an unusual tale, the Caliph was not at all surprised, but rather had his soldiers bring to him the husband, who turned out to be the Caliph's own son. This they did, and the second young woman (rather shockingly) did *not* forgive him, though people often did in those days.

But from the third he learned nothing. She only smiled and offered a respectful bow, requesting that the Caliph honor the precept of the house in which he had stayed: to ask not about that which did not concern him.

This only intrigued the Caliph more. But the women had given him hospitality; he had rewarded the first with the restoration of her sisters, and the second with the punishment of her husband. How could he reward the third, except to grant her request?

Because the Caliph was not only a virtuous man but an amorous one, he found an additional way. He offered to wed the third woman, and she accepted, and this is where the story customarily ends.

It is not quite true to say the Caliph knew nothing about his beautiful new wife. The three women of that strange household were half-sisters—daughters of the same father—and so from the other two he knew that piece of his wife's heritage. He knew that by the standards of the harem she was neither the most beautiful nor the least, and that she was pious enough to suit his requirements. He knew she could dance and tell stories.

But she did not tell him her own.

Time and again the question tugged at his tongue, begging to be asked. He bestowed upon her gifts of emeralds and fine silk, sweets of sesame or lemon, a trained monkey to amuse her in the long afternoons. She smiled and laughed and thanked him, yet she did not share her tale. He made sure she had friends in the harem, women who would be her companions and confidantes, yet she did not share her tale. He offered her freedom if she wished it, a house and wealth enough to live out the rest of her days; she declined, and did not share her tale.

And the Caliph never asked. He had promised, and although he was clever enough to sometimes find ways of escaping the bonds of his promises, he could not escape this one. He had offered to wed her not because of her past, for that, he did not know; he therefore could not rightly claim that this information was his concern, when he had not been concerned with it before. He did not even know her name, calling her only by the name given to her in the harem, which was Nour.

"How can her past not concern you?" cried his vizier. He asked this question many times over the following years, though never in public, where it might shame the Caliph. "She could be a jinniyah! Or the slave of some wicked sorcerer! Or a sorceress herself!"

The Caliph considered all these explanations quite possible, for in those days, nothing was more likely. He said, "If she is a jinniyah, perhaps she is cursed to expiate some past sin by living a hundred human lives, and if she tells anyone of this, her expiation will begin anew. If she is the slave of some wicked sorcerer, perhaps her mother or her brother is his prisoner, and if she divulges the smallest part of her identity, the sorcerer will kill his captive. If she herself is a sorceress, skilled in many strange arts from foreign lands, perhaps she fears that if she admits this I will strike her head from her shoulders in a rage."

"As well you should," muttered his vizier. Protecting the safety of the Caliph was one of his duties; he felt, not without reason, that he could not fully execute this duty when a total stranger enjoyed such intimate privileges with his master. And he harbored a deep suspicion that this last mystery was the most dangerous of them all.

But the Caliph had given his word. And though some days the question beat so strongly within his heart that he feared it would leap from his mouth of its own accord, in time a captive bird grows habituated to its cage; and so it was with his curiosity. Years went by, and her tale remained untold.

Until a time came, as it always does, when the Destroyer of all earthly pleasures, the Annihilator of men, drew close to the Caliph's side.

This came much sooner than anyone might have wished, for the Caliph was not yet an old man. His beard had only a little grey in it, and had his health continued strong, he might have ruled for many years still. But such things are the will of Allah, not of men, and Harun al-Rashid knew his end was near.

By then he found more comfort in the company of the wife called Nour than in any other of his harem. Her undisclosed tale, which had once been a burr beneath his foot, an ant inside his silken robe, a constant irritation and distraction, had instead become a source of odd serenity. Others among his wives troubled him with their past problems and present relations and future ambitions, but not this one. She kept her own counsel, and that soothed him.

One day as he lay at rest, the sandalwood windows adding their fragrance to the cooling breeze, she brushed a strand of hair from his brow and said, "You have never asked me about my past."

"It does not concern me," the Caliph murmured sleepily. He had said it many times before, though usually to his vizier.

She said, "I have listened to storytellers from far-off lands as well as our own. They tell countless tales of people who gave their word and then broke it, people who did the single thing they were asked or commanded not to do. They spilled secrets; they opened doors and boxes; they struck their wives three times. I sometimes think that you alone, in all the world, are capable of remaining true."

The Caliph said nothing, but he closed his eyes as she continued to stroke his brow.

After a moment his wife said, "My husband, I never told you my tale because there was nothing to tell. We live in a time of daily wonders, where fishermen become sultans and jinn whisk people to the far corners of the earth in the blink of an eye. From my eldest half-sister you heard how she traveled to an island where all the people had been turned to black stone save one devout prince, only to see him killed by her treacherous full sisters, those selfsame dogs you watched her beat. From my middle half-sister you heard how she thought she was paying a visit of charity to a penniless household, only to find herself in a sumptuous palace, wedding the selfsame man who later beat her almost to death because another man talked her into enduring an unwanted kiss on the cheek. You heard how three separate dervishes were blinded in the same eye due to different improbable confluences of circumstances, which are the most probable of things in this world of ours.

"But I? I have no such tale. I have lived an unremarkable life. I command no jinn, nor have I ever been the captive of a wicked sorcerer. I have not even poisoned the evil brother of my late husband, who thought to marry me after committing fratricide, for you are the only husband I have ever had.

"I am an ordinary woman, the sort whose tale is rarely remembered. But you, my husband, are an extraordinary man, for you made me a promise and kept it. And in both this world of ours and the world that will later be—a world in which jinn and sorcerers and rocs stealing men away to the tops of the tallest mountains will no longer be commonplace occurrences—that is the most wondrous thing of all."

By the time she was done speaking, and perhaps even before that, the Caliph had fallen asleep. Which was a thing men often did in those days, and still do today; we will not fault him for it. The wife who was content to be called Nour bent to kiss him, and let him sleep.

EAST ASIAN

Centuries of Kings

I HAVE KILLED kings, lured emperors to their doom; destroyed courts, brought countries to war; for thousands of years I have brought chaos with me wherever I go, death not enough to stop me, and I regret none of it.

And now the hunters pursue me through the wood.

Tamamo-no-Mae. Pao Si. Dakki. These are but a few of the names I have answered to in my life. Wife, concubine, whore. I have answered to these as well. Two thousand years is a long time—more than one name can bear.

They blur together in my mind, the kings I have killed. Few last for more than a year, and then I move on. Not all have been kings. But men of power, yes; the poor or unimportant do not interest me. I go from land to land—China, India, Japan—where I am does not matter to me so much as who I find there. Toba is the most recent, but it began with Zhou.

I remember the days in Zhou's court as if they were yesterday, though they lie centuries distant. The court of the last Emperor of the Shang Dynasty, the man said to be more dissolute than any other in China. I could tell such tales of that court—tell of the day he demanded that seventy-two ladies of the highest blood strip to their skin and dance, in public, for his entertainment. When they refused, he had a ditch dug before his palace, and he filled it with snakes and lizards and biting insects; when it was full his guards threw the women into the ditch, and their screams filled the air. And he laughed and asked if I did not find it amusing.

I found my amusement elsewhere. A few words in the right ears, and trouble was seeded; you cannot murder seventy-two ladies of the highest blood and not expect rebellion in response. Zhou expected it, but his arrogance had robbed him of allies. His enemies stormed the palace compound late one night, and he died in his favorite pavilion, perishing amid the flames.

The fire did not begin outside, with the invaders. It began inside, from a tipped lamp.

I died in that fire with him, but by then it did not matter; I was finished with Zhou.

This much I will say for the hunters: they are noble men. Many have chased me in their time, but few have been as distinguished as Miura-no-Suke Yoshiaki and Kazusa-no-Suke Hirotsune. Retired Emperor Toba set them on my heels, and they are determined, more determined than many who have gone before them. This is the third time they have pursued me. The first time, I gave them the slip, and the second, their horses faltered before I did. Again they return, though, and now we flit through the hills and woods of Shimotsuke-no-Kuni, across the Nasu Plain, our feet as swift as leaves driven by the wind.

They may catch me; they may kill me. It does not matter. However many times I die, I will always find my way back.

I returned to China years later, during the dynasty called Zhou. Not the same name, but it echoed nonetheless with memories of snakes and screams. The Emperor then was Yu, twelfth of his line, who cast aside another woman for me. He wanted to make me smile: a harmless enough goal. But flowers and jewels brought no light to my face; the antics of monkeys and dogs were to me as indifferent as the changing of the moon.

Could he have succeeded, had he known how to pursue his goal? Years had passed since my time in Zhou's court, true, but not so many—not nearly so many as have passed now. Perhaps I could have smiled, then, for some cause other than bitterness or vengeful amusement. Perhaps.

But that was centuries ago, and who can say now what might have been?

A court functionary suggested it to him. Yu lit the signal-fires, meant to summon soldiers to him in case of need. The soldiers rushed to the courtyard, all in haste, and when I saw them there....

I laughed.

Yu misunderstood. He heard in that laugh nothing of harm. But I saw the soldiers milling over the paving-stones, and I heard the angry mutters of the lords, and I saw that Yu was a fool, and that his foolishness would bring him down. It was for *that* I laughed.

He saw me laugh, and was pleased; and, as I had known he would, he lit the signal-fires again and again, all for my sake, and every time I laughed louder.

I laughed the loudest of all when the father of the woman Yu had cast aside returned with an army, and he lit the signal fires one final time.

I laughed, not because the soldiers came, but because they did not. And Yu perished alone.

I do not know where the two noble hunters found their horses; these are not the ones they rode before. They pursue me without pausing, thundering across the plain toward the peaks of the Nasu Mountains, and although I am swift, I cannot outrun them.

Fools. This chase is for nothing. Toba will perish. And so may I, it is true; but that will accomplish nothing save to make these noble warriors feel proud. They will congratulate each other, and return home, and be given the feast of heroes—but they cannot stop the cycle, nor turn it back.

They cannot undo the past. No one can.

Zhou set this in motion two thousand years ago. Let them blame *him*, if they will.

☙

Some kings I bring down through war or rebellion; others waste away. So it was with the Retired Emperor Toba. I was a mere servant-girl when he first cast his eye upon me, but such considerations did not stop him; my beauty was unsurpassed, my hair a shining river of blackness, my skin as perfect and pale as the moon, and the scent of my body was never marred by sweat or dirt. In darkness, I glowed with my own light.

That much was obvious to see. The rest, he discovered with time. We listened to music, and I amazed him with my knowledge of it. We viewed the moon, and my poems were gems, more precious than any the others could compose. He questioned me on Buddhist teachings, and found my answers wise beyond even his comprehension.

Two thousand years is a long time. I have learned much, and forgotten nothing.

Toba sickened before long. But someone in his cloistered court had more sense than most; someone dispatched a messenger to summon the great diviner Abe no Yasuchika to the Sendo Palace. Many of that kind are frauds, but Yasuchika had eyes that saw much, and when he turned those eyes upon the emperor's sickness he saw what I had done.

Oh, indeed, he saw much. But not all.

He saw the life draining from the emperor, draining from him to me. He saw my pointed ears, my golden fur, my nine tails. He saw the centuries of slaughter stretching behind me.

But he did not see where it began.

They chased me from the palace with dogs and bows, sent warriors to hunt me down. The word echoed in the halls of the Sendo Palace: *kitsune!* And I fled, abandoning my human mask, flying over hills in the form of a fox.

Yasuchika never guessed what he failed to see. He never saw the playful young fox spirit that once lived in China, free from care. He looked away too soon, and did not see an emperor take interest in her; nor did he see her fox-father refuse, knowing too well the corruption of humans.

Yasuchika closed his eyes, and did not watch as the great Shang Emperor Zhou, noble and wise, with the mandate of heaven behind him—a foolish, human conceit!—sent his soldiers to take the fox against her will.

That is where it began. But this, Yasuchika did not see. For he believed he had seen enough.

We have reached the base of the mountains, the noble hunters and I. My strength is at its end. Soon they will catch me, and then I will die.

I have died before. I no longer fear it. Toba will die as well, and that is all I ask for now.

Zhou is dead; Yu is dead; Toba will soon join them. The names of those I have brought down form a list whose recital would last hours. I take pride in that list, as I take pride in little else. What is beauty to me, or immortality, or the nine tails I have earned? What are love, joy, peace? These inner things, valued things, were taken from me long ago, and the outward things matter not at all. What matters is that Zhou has paid, and Yu has paid, and Toba will soon pay for *his* own crimes.

Oh, I heard what the ladies-in-waiting said, whispering in the corridors of the Sendo Palace as Toba weakened and moaned. He is a good man, they said. A wise ruler, guiding the country from behind the throne, retiring out of the light of court so he may concentrate on more important things.

Perhaps it is so. But his crimes would have come soon enough. They always do.

I learned that lesson from Zhou, centuries ago. Humans are of two kinds: mindless cattle, and the iron-fisted tyrants who herd and devour them. Those without power, and those who abuse the power they have.

Toba had power, and in time he would have used it for evil. For that, I have delivered justice. It is what I do.

The arrows thud into the dirt around me. I dart and leap,

changing direction, but as I slip between the trees, I see something flash by.

A slip of paper, tied to the branch of a tree.

I realize at last that this chase has been different. My hunters have been herdsmen, leading me to this trap. Enchantment forms a net around me, and behind it I feel the hand of Yasu-chika. He will bring his holiness to bear against me, Buddhist prayers, Shinto charms, and perhaps this is how I will die.

Holy men have killed me before.

The hunters pull their horses up short, shouting words I cannot hear. The chanting of Yasuchika fills my ears, and now, too late, too late, I feel what he is doing.

He will not kill me. He will do worse.

My hind paws drag in the dirt, cease to move. I cannot lift them. I rear up and am frozen thus, held by the trap I entered so carelessly. I curse this blind monk, who does not see that what I do is right and good, that it is *necessary*. He calls me an *oni*, a demon, and now he will bind me to this spot. My body grows heavy and stiff. I cannot move. He has caught me well, stealing my freedom, my ability to transform, leaving me on the edge of the Nasu Plain as nothing more than a twisted stone.

He won that day, and he lost.

The diviner put an end to my centuries of kings. He trapped me in this body of stone.

But my spirit survives.

Now my victims must come to me, and I care no more for justice. They call me the Death Stone, the Murderer Stone, an object filled with malice and hate. Those who understand avoid me, but there are always the strangers, the travelers, the ignorant.

The fools.

The enchantment that put me here will not last forever. Someday it will wane, and I will break free once more. There will be no mercy for the humans then. I will kill them as I find them, draining out their life, and no monk babbling prayers will trap me, ever again.

For I have learned the lesson of Zhou, the lesson of Yasuchika. Power is what matters, not the use to which it is put. I was a fool to think otherwise. I am a demon indeed, and will bring hell to them on earth.

The Old Woman and the Tea

WHEN THE SOLDIERS arrive, the old woman is waiting.

"Sit down, sit down," she urges them, gesturing with her free hand. There are cushions spread on the floor, one for each soldier. "The tea will be ready soon."

The soldiers grip their rifles. Their leader says, "Old Lady Meng, we are here to—"

"I know why you're here. That's no reason not to be polite. Didn't your parents teach you any manners? Sit."

They sit. The water approaches boiling, and she removes it from the fire before it can slip across that line. With a bamboo whisk, she stirs in five different ingredients. None of them look quite like tea leaves.

"We will drink together," she says as the brew steeps, "and then you can carry out your duty."

They're Red Guards, these men with their rifles. Their duty is to destroy the Four Olds, the shackles of ossified tradition holding China back from her glorious future. All these soldiers know of religion is that it's one of the tools the ruling class use to oppress the proletariat. That's all they need to know: They've been assigned to deal with this old woman, and a good soldier doesn't ask questions.

Elsewhere, there's a war on. Much bigger detachments of soldiers have been sent after the Queen Mother of the West, Guan Yu, the Monkey King. Those deities will fight back. The Monkey King might even win.

But one old woman?

They accept their bowls of tea. They sip. They smile.

It's a pleasure to rest like this, in an empty house, away from prying eyes. These men may be devoted their duty, but they're still human, and every human likes to take a break once in a while, in those rare moments between assignments. Their commanding officer will contact them soon enough, with the name of another god to hunt down and kill. For now they relax, taking their ease while they have nothing to do.

Rain begins to fall as the old woman slips away. It smells a little odd—a bit like leaves and flowers, like something people drank once, but they can't recall when or where. They'll lick the water from their lips, brows furrowing as they try to summon it to mind; then they'll shake their heads and go about their lives in the bright, bloody world of Chairman Mao's China.

Salt mingles with the rain on Old Lady Meng's face, slipping from the corners of her eyes. She will survive the Chairman's revolution, when so many others are destroyed or reduced to a shadow of their former selves. Sacrifices on the altar of progress. She will live, and preserve the others in her heart.

But her survival has a price. No one will ever fully recall her glory now. Just a minor underworld deity, assigned to serve the Waters of Oblivion that wash souls clean of memory before their reincarnation. Most will not even recognize her name.

Old Lady Meng will remember—and be forgotten.

Ghost and Fox

IT WAS TO be expected, the doctor said, after such a close call as yours. He spoke in learned terms of excesses of yin, of meridians and flows, stagnation in the blood that he had put right. The woman they said was your mother listened and nodded and paid him with taels of silver, thanking him with her forehead to the floor. She loved you, that was clear—loved you enough to spend a small fortune saving you.

Saving your life, at least. *A simpleton now,* the neighbors said, wagging their heads in regret. *She'll never be married. Such a shame. But some kind-hearted man might take her for his concubine.*

You weren't meant to overhear their words. And you didn't hear what came after, because memory overwhelmed you: hands caressing your breasts, fever-warm against your cold skin, and heat flooding into you like the light of the sun itself.

Then it faded. You were the daughter of a wealthy family, sheltered behind high walls. No man could possibly have gotten that close to you.

You believed them when they said your near-fatal illness had made you simple. After all, you didn't remember your mother, your father, the house you awoke in. Your own childhood nurse was a stranger. You ate what they gave you and stood like an obedient doll when they dressed you, because no one believed you could manage anything for yourself.

But your mind wasn't weak. You carried on conversations, read books your Second Brother brought you. The past was a blank, but you remembered new things without trouble.

You lied to them all.

The past wasn't a blank. It was a bottomless pool of strange recollections, into which you hardly dared dip more than your toes, for fear you would fall into its depths and drown. A house that was not the one you lived in. A slipper too small for your foot. Poems you had never read, songs you had never sung; you eyed your Third Sister's zither and suspected that if you set your hand to the strings, you could play it better than she did—though everyone said you had never been musical.

The word for that wasn't "simple." It was "mad."

Your family saw your distress, and did what they could to set it right. The countryside, they reasoned, would be gentler for your weakened body and mind than the clamor of the city. They sent you to live in a rural house with your old nurse and your Second Brother to watch over you.

Out there, at least, you weren't surrounded by things you were expected to remember and didn't. Accompanied by your Second Brother and the things you shouldn't remember but did, you went for short walks in the fields, watching birds flit from branch to branch and foxes dart into the undergrowth. It brought a kind of peace.

Until you reached the tomb by the side of the road. Then you began to scream and scream, and your Second Brother carried you home, sending your nurse to fetch a doctor to sedate you. But he was not as skilled as the one in the city, and so even when you sank down into dreams, you could not escape the truth: that the weed-haunted tomb was once your own.

There was a time when I hated you.

Such a selfish little ghost, draining the yang energy from my beloved Sang with night after night of love-making, when I had been so cautious. I wanted to stay by his side always, but the danger to him was too great; I made myself stay away, visiting only when I could bear the separation no longer. You, though— you thought only of the love and pleasure the two of you shared. And so you fed on him, until he nearly died. I would have killed you for that, except you were already dead.

When I caught you, though…how could I hate one whose love mirrored my own so well? And you were willing to do anything to save him. Even if it risked your own existence.

When you disappeared, I had everything I thought I wanted: Sang all to myself, with no competition, and my own self-restraint to keep him safe. Only when you were gone did I realize you had become as dear to me as he is.

Do you think it mere chance that he has come to this house and asked for your hand in marriage? There were only two possibilities for what had become of you. One was that some Buddhist monk or Taoist priest had banished you for good, sending your restless spirit onward. The other…

Everyone was gossiping. The daughter of the Zhang family, making such a miraculous recovery, when even the doctor thought she would die. Some even whispered she *had* died, and the doctor brought her back to life. He never confirmed it, but he smiles whenever anyone asks him, because a physician who can revive the dead commands very high fees indeed.

It had nothing to do with him, and everything to do with a wandering spirit and a body freshly vacated.

You did not remember your family because they were never yours to begin with. The memories you could not explain were your own. And so was the tomb.

It took a lot of gossiping where your so-called mother would overhear before I persuaded them to send you to the country. You needed to know the truth, before Sang presented himself at the Zhang family door. If you hadn't strolled in the right direction that morning, I would have contrived to point you there eventually. And if the tomb did not spark your memories, I would have tried other tactics, until you understood.

Now the path is clear. You are a ghost no more; Sang can come to your bed without fear. Once the negotiations with your supposed father are complete, you will return to his house as his flesh-and-blood wife.

Do not embrace me yet, dear sister-in-love. I am the one who is a danger now, to you as well as him. My self-restraint is not as perfect as I might wish, and I would never forgive myself if my touch hurt either of you.

But be patient. It is not so common as ghosts restored to life, but there are tales of fox spirits reincarnating in human form. I will find a way. And when I have, I will return to you and to Sang, and the three of us will live together again—no longer ghost and fox and victim, but alive, and human, and happy for the rest of our days.

Speak to the Moon

IN NISHINA CRATER, silence.

Inside the Kaguya 6 lander, Itō's voice, reading off the vehicle's current power, fuel stores, oxygen tanks, and more.

On Tanegashima Island, hundreds of thousands of kilometers away, dozens of other voices doing the same, in the calm tone of accountants checking their figures.

In Kemuriyama's heart, a poem.

He recorded his co-pilot's observations like an automaton, respecting the needs of the moment, but his lips shaped the soundless words. And when Itō paused, Kemuriyama's gaze slid sideways, to the lander's viewports. They showed nothing but dust, kicked up by the retro-rockets.

Six hours. Waiting for that glowing haze to settle, for all the preparatory steps to be done. Six hours before they could begin the work for which they'd been sent here.

He shook that thought away. The work was going on right now, as he relayed Itō's numbers to Hashimoto in the command module high above the surface of the Moon and Hashimoto in turn verified them with JAXA's mission control. The steady trade of data masked an underlying sea of excitement: Japan had joined the select company of nations that had sent a crewed lander to the Moon. And not by riding the coattails of the Americans or the Russians or the Chinese, using other countries' launch sites and experts, but on their own.

They each acknowledged the significance in their own way. When the immediate tasks of landing were complete, Itō unclipped her harness and stood in the Moon's reduced gravity, then bowed deeply to Kemuriyama. "Thank you. It is because of the efforts of you and your family that we have come this far."

He freed himself and stood to return her bow. It wasn't quite like it had been in the training pool; air didn't resist him the way water did. The lightness of his body felt dreamlike, as if he were on the verge of leaving his flesh behind. "This achievement belongs to us all," he said. "One man could not do this on his own—not even if he tried for a thousand years."

Her formality bent into a smile. "I suppose you have a poem for the occasion."

"A trivial thing," Kemuriyama said. "My skill has never been great."

"You're the best poet at JAXA," Itō said, politely not mentioning that he had very little competition. "Let's hear it."

Kemuriyama bent his head for a moment, then recited:

> *A stalk of bamboo*
> *once joined the earth and the moon*
> *for a fleeting time—*
> *the fires of our engines*
> *are no more lasting a bridge.*

Itō nodded. "Kaguya-hime. Very fitting—if not very cheerful." The folktale was familiar to everyone at JAXA; they'd been naming lunar craft after it since 2007. Hashimoto's command module was Taketori, the Bamboo-Cutter, who'd found Kaguya-hime and raised her as his radiant, otherworldly daughter. Kemuriyama had tried to argue for something different, but he had been overruled.

Itō craned her neck at one of the viewports, studying the dust. Then she sighed—a rare show of impatience—and helped Kemuriyama reconfigure the interior of the lander for work. After that they were under orders to rest for a few hours, and Kemuriyama obediently lay down and composed himself.

But he didn't sleep, and when he rose a little while later to retrieve a small, hard-sided case, the glint of Itō's half-open eyes told him she, too, was incapable of slumber.

It meant he didn't have to worry about disturbing her. Kemuriyama knelt on the floor of the lander and laid out a towel, then unlatched the case. The bottle of water inside was from Ise Grand Shrine. It poured slowly in the reduced lunar gravity, sliding over his hands like a caress. First the left, then the right; then a small sip from his left palm, rinsed around his mouth and spat out, before he cleansed that hand once more. The towel absorbed it all.

"The Moon is not a land to be conquered, nor a resource to be exploited," he'd said when he presented his request to the mission planners. "Showing respect to the Moon will remind us to behave respectfully while we are there." The mission planners hadn't argued. The monitors in the control center on Tanegashima were decorated with prayer strips from Matsu-no-o Taisha, where Tsukuyomi-no-Mikoto, the kami of the moon, was enshrined. No one in the space program, be they Shinto, Buddhist, Christian, or atheist, saw any harm in a few reassurances.

Ideally Kemuriyama would have performed his purification outside, but on this point the laws of nature were inflexible. In the vacuum of space, the water would boil away in a matter of seconds. He had to make do.

He re-capped the bottle and returned it to his case, then wrung out the towel in their tiny bathing chamber. By the time he emerged, Itō had risen and was at the controls, opening the protective shell that covered his suitport.

Despite her bow and her words of gratitude, he knew she was a little bitter. The Kemuriyama family had supplemented JAXA's funding for decades, which in Itō's eyes put him into the category of "rich tourist" rather than "true astronaut." It grated with her that he should be the first Japanese person to set foot on the lunar surface. But Kemuriyama was fully trained for this mission, and generations of support, scientific as well as monetary, earned him the right to request this honor.

Itō was too professional to say anything regardless, when all their conversations were being recorded. She'd only spoken of it once, drunkenly, after the decision was made. Now she merely ran the checks on his suit, then came to help him into it. A person on her own could step into the suit and seal it with help from the lander's systems; that was one of the things Kemuriyama had worked to develop. It was easier with assistance, though, and safer. And he appreciated the gesture.

When the suit was fully sealed, Itō's voice came over the speaker. "*Ganbatte.*" Not "good luck" as people said in English, but an exhortation to do his best.

"Yes," Kemuriyama said, and detached from the lander.

Most of the dust had settled, coaxed down by the Moon's slight gravity. More puffed up as his boots sank into the powdery surface. Kemuriyama took a few gentle, bounding strides, testing his mobility. Then he turned around and found Itō had opened the airlock for him. Inside, his case waited.

Soon enough they would begin the tasks for which JAXA had sent them here. An un-crewed mission had already dropped the crates containing the materials for the radio telescope they were to build here on the far side of the Moon; he could see them a short distance away. But before that, he had a ritual to finish. Purification was only the first step, just as donning his suit was only the beginning of an EVA.

He had no need of a shrine. Like a mountain, the Moon itself could be sacred, divine power manifest in the physical world.

Kemuriyama bowed twice, then clapped his gloves together. That was meant to attract the attention of the kami, but here on the airless surface of the Moon, where no sound could carry, the only noise was the faint thudding within his suit. He bowed again, hoping it would suffice.

Then he opened the case and laid out his offering. The branch of green sakaki leaves withered and seared instantly as its moisture boiled away, but the folded paper streamers attached to it danced in the low gravity as he turned the branch and laid it reverently on the ground.

The words he spoke then had been given to him by the senior priest at Matsu-no-o Taisha, a prayer to Tsukuyomi-no-Mikoto and the other kami of the moon. He was not and never had been a priest himself. But in his heart, he added his own prayer.

May I find here the beauty I lost so long ago.

The days after that were too busy to allow him much time for thought. Many components of the radio telescope had been constructed ahead of time, but assembling the various parts into a working whole still required a great deal of attentive, painstaking effort. And although Itō might have been annoyed that Kemuriyama had won the honor of being the first to step out onto the Moon, being the second was no small thing. Her mood improved, and before long they were trading jokes with Hashimoto up in the command module.

There were a few small problems and delays, but the schedule had been designed with that inevitability in mind. Itō and Kemuriyama finished up in good time, and she showed no sign of lingering resentment when she helped him into his suit on the final day.

He'd purified himself again, and now made another offering to the kami, thanking them and apologizing for the disruption this mission had brought. When he was done, he set the case down at the base of the airlock ramp and took a deep breath, tasting the chemical-tinged air of his suit.

If he was wrong, he would not have long to regret his mistake. But that, in its own way, would be all right.

He looked up at the camera that recorded his movements outside and bowed deeply. In formal language, he said, "There is no excuse for the inconvenience I am about to cause. I have left an explanation in my locker at Tanegashima; I know it will most likely create as much confusion as it will resolve. I offer my sincerest apologies for the difficulties that will result from my actions. But I made a promise a very long time ago, and I must keep it."

Over the radio, he heard Itō's voice. "Eh? What are you talking about, Kemuri-kun?"

His answer came without words. He reached up to the neck of his EVA suit, found the latch for his helmet, and released it.

The hiss of air escaping didn't quite drown out the sudden flood of curses from Itō as she realized what he was doing. Even after his helmet was gone, the vibration of his earpiece against his skull told him she was still talking. But once he removed that, he was in utter silence as he methodically stripped off his EVA suit and placed it at the base of the ramp. The equipment was custom-built for each astronaut; still, taking it with him would feel like stealing. Perhaps they could get further use out of it somehow. Itō could put on her own gear and retrieve it—but suiting up on her own, while possible, would be slower. She wouldn't be clear of the suitport before he was gone.

She might chase him anyway. Here on the Moon, with no wind to disturb his footprints, he would leave a clear trail. But he hoped the sight of him standing on the airless lunar surface, wearing nothing more than his inner suit, would dissuade her from trying. She had to get back to the command module soon anyway, or else ruin the mission plan and condemn both herself and Hashimoto to death.

Itō was a practical woman. He had confidence she would make the right choice.

Kemuriyama picked up his case and stepped back from the lander. He bowed again.

Then he walked away, across the surface of the Moon.

The worst part wasn't the pain: the boiling away of all surface moisture, the swelling of his skin at the loss of pressure, the excruciating ache in his joints as decompression sickness set in. He'd experienced a lack of air before—when he tried to drown himself, hang himself, kill himself in a hundred different ways—and the searing temperature of the sunlit surface felt no worse than standing too close to a fire.

No, the worst part was the silence. It pressed upon him like a weight. He could not tell whether, in the absence of all other sound, he truly could hear the internal movements of his body, the bending of his joints and the flex and stretch of his muscles… or whether he was hallucinating it, the way someone in a dark room might hallucinate light. It made him want to scream, just to alleviate the tension, but he had no air to give him voice.

Instead he composed a poem, imagining the sound of his own voice, the black strokes of the calligraphy.

> *Light passes across*
> *the stones and dust of the Moon*
> *and changes nothing;*
> *the suffering of the flesh*
> *is just as impermanent.*

He walked steadily, not looking back at the lander receding in the distance. He'd studied maps of the Moon for a long time, ever since the Black Ships arrived in Edo Bay and opened Japan to the outside world, after centuries of isolation. In their wake had come western science and western technology—including telescopes. In those days he hadn't expected anything to come of it, but he'd gazed through the lenses at the silver disk in the sky, night after long night.

Then came western fiction. Jules Verne, *De la Terre à la Lune*, and later its sequel, *Autour de la Lune*. He'd learned French in order to be able to read them. Then English, to read stories about square-jawed men with ray guns fighting bug-eyed aliens in outer space.

He wasn't the only one who read such things and wondered if it might be possible. He'd hardly slept during the three weeks when Sputnik 1 orbited the Earth. Afterward, he found out that men at Tokyo University were experimenting with rockets: one of several early projects that grew into various government agencies, and eventually into JAXA.

It was in 1960 that he decided: *I will go to the Moon.*

But with the wounds of World War II only half-healed, he feared he wouldn't be accepted into the United States' space program. Nor were the Soviets any more likely to take him. Besides, it felt wrong to abandon his country for another—a betrayal of the man he once served. Instead he fixed his attention on Japan's own agencies. Under the name Kemuriyama Hideo, he began to study aeronautics, astrophysics, anything he could use to further his goal.

When too many years had passed, he sank quietly into obscurity, then came back as his own son, Kemuriyama Shigeru.

Generation by generation, step by step. A crewed lunar mission wasn't the most useful thing JAXA might do, but the Keguriyama family had worked so hard, donated so much money, believed so strongly in that goal. And there was still cachet in the achievement, even if people's attention was mostly on Mars these days.

He truly did regret the difficulties he had now caused them. What would they do with the explanation he'd left behind? Cover it up, most likely; swear everyone to secrecy and create some story to explain his tragic death. The truth would leak out, but it would be the stuff of tabloids. Conspiracy theorists would pore over satellite images of the Moon and tell themselves they saw signs of his presence.

That was fine. He was used to people telling stories about him. The only difference now would be that he had become the main character, instead of a nameless figure at the end.

He'd plotted a course a man could follow on foot, across the crags and plains of the far side of the Moon. It took him out of sight of the lander as fast as possible, so that Itō wouldn't be tormented for too long by the impossible sight of him. But after that his only purpose was to keep moving, to cover as much ground as he could.

One direction was as good as another, when he could not be sure where his destination lay.

People had once thought they saw canals on Mars, but nobody claimed anything like that for the Moon. It was uninhabited, and uninhabitable. If there had been any signs of people, cities, any kind of life, someone would have found it long since.

Perhaps there was nothing. Perhaps the people who once lived here—not bug-eyed and green-skinned, but radiant and beautiful—left a long time ago, before humanity invented telescopes.

If that was the case, then he would walk until his will gave out, and then he would find someplace to hide where he could not be seen by satellites. Eventually someone might find him, if they did not all go to Mars instead…but in the meanwhile, he would have peace. He was even coming to terms with the silence.

But the people of the moon were not bound by human science. If a girl no bigger than a thumb could be found inside a stalk of bamboo, if a man could live for a thousand years and more, then anything was possible. Even a civilization on an airless rock, invisible to watching eyes.

He walked toward the Sun, chasing it with his bounding, lightweight strides. The only names he had for features on the Moon were those given by human beings; those could not tell him where to search. He went sunward because he dreaded the darkness, at least a little. Without the Sun's light, the temperature would plummet, and he hadn't been able to determine what that would do to his body. Not kill him, he suspected—if he wasn't dead now, then a mere hundred some-odd degrees Celsius below zero would not do it—but it might slow him down. Then, like a mechanical rover, he would need to wait for the return of the light before he could continue his search.

He'd waited countless lifetimes for this, and yet he found he could still be impatient.

Even with the reduced gravity to speed his progress, though, he couldn't outrun the night. It crept up behind him, blanketing the lunar surface in darkness, a crisp line in the absence of an atmosphere to diffuse it. As it drew close, he set his case down on a nearby rock and opened it once more.

A foolish gesture, perhaps. But the people of the moon had not come out to greet him, and he might search for another thousand years without ever finding where they hid. His only hope was to ask for a guide, here on the boundary between day and night.

The last thing in the case was a small, vacuum-stiffened ball of mochi.

He laid it atop another rock. The airless void robbed him of his voice, but in his mind, he called out: begging Tsukuyomi-no-Mikoto for his favor and aid, praying to the kami of the moon to send him a divine messenger.

Westerners looked at the Moon and saw a man's face in it. Japanese people saw a rabbit. And the rabbit, they said, was pounding mochi.

As the last of the light slipped out from under him, he crouched in the dust and used his finger to write out another poem.

> *This old mochi ball,*
> *like the prayer in my heart,*
> *   is long past its prime,*
> *but may these small offerings*
> *retain some trace of fragrance.*

Then he folded himself into a kneeling position, set his hands on his knees, and let the night take him.

Without his suit, he had no way to measure time. But he knew the numbers by heart: A lunar synodic day was twenty-nine and a half terrestrial days long. Half that time was spent in darkness, and half in light.

Fourteen and three-quarters days in darkness, with only his heartbeat and the stars to mark its passage. He could not even focus on his breath, for he had none.

Two weeks to wonder if he'd made a terrible mistake. If he should have pushed for a mission to the Moon's Earth-facing side instead. Two weeks to calculate how long it would take him to walk there across the cratered lunar surface, while in the mean-time his body ached and his joints stiffened and froze.

An eternity of waiting. But he was used to that.

Then, as the Sun's fire raced across the ground toward him, the rabbit appeared.

Small and furred, its ears pricked in curiosity, exactly like any rabbit found on Earth.

It hopped through the dust in this airless, lifeless place, toward the frozen lump of mochi he had set out.

He would have sobbed in relief, if he'd had breath to do it with. Because the rabbit was the first sign that he might not be wrong: that he hadn't stranded himself in a place he could never return from, with no hope of success; that there was something here other than barren stone and the detritus of humanity's exploration.

The rabbit stopped and sniffed the non-existent air. He remained still, lest he frighten it off. It bounded up the stone, moving as if Earth's own gravity tied it down, and extended its twitching nose toward the mochi.

As the line of dawn swept over them both, the rabbit thumped one hind foot against the ground—and the world changed.

Towers rose around him, translucent and green as fine jade. They were neither the pagodas of Japanese tradition, nor the techno-logical marvels of science fictional speculation; they soared like bamboo in the slight gravity of the Moon, impossibly graceful and tall. They caught the light of the stars and refracted it, so the avenues of the endless lunar city glittered like the heavens themselves.

At the sight, air hissed into his frozen, disused lungs.

He collapsed forward, retching, shuddering from head to foot. *Air.* He'd never been so grateful for it, not even when he spent a week at the bottom of the sea, hoping that if he was patient enough he would drown.

When he raised his head, he was not alone.

He'd seen their kind before, more than a thousand years ago, when they came to bring their errant daughter home. Tall, radiant, their skin the gold of sunlight, their hair the black of the space between the stars. Their beauty was almost painful to look on. Their fury…that, he discovered, was worse.

But they didn't raise a hand against him. They only stood, staring, at the human being who had somehow come into their world.

He leaned forward carefully, easing the stiffness of vacuum's cold out of his body, bowing until his head touched the lunar soil. "Please forgive me the rudeness of my intrusion," he said, with all the formality he could bring to bear. "I come in search of Kaguya-hime."

From his prison, he could see the Earth.

Green and blue and white, waxing and waning, glowing against the velvet darkness of space like the tide jewels of ancient legend. He wrote poetry to it, the way he had once written poetry for moon-viewing parties. Itō would not have liked any of his compositions. She didn't understand the beauty of ephemerality. But the Earth had never seemed more precious to him than now, when he would likely never set foot on it again.

His prison had no walls. Only a door like a lattice of curling vines, where the platform on which he sat joined to one of the tall spires in the endless, luminescent city. He could step off at any time. The gravity was still slight, but the fall would be enough to shatter him—to kill him, if he could die. He was almost tempted to try it. But he still had hope that Kaguya-hime might come.

As the lunar day stretched onward, though, that hope wavered. The people of the moon spoke a different tongue amongst themselves, a language like the whispering of a solar wind; perhaps they didn't understand his request. Perhaps they'd forgotten all about her sojourn on Earth. Perhaps she had a different name now. Perhaps she was dead.

No—not that last. Her parting letter had made him certain of that much.

The day was ebbing, night's veil drawing over some of the distant towers. He stood and paced to the edge of his prison, looking down at the ground and the people far below.

When he turned back, someone stood on the other side of the vine-lattice door.

Even after so long, he had not forgotten the perfection of that face.

"Kaguya-hime," he breathed. Kneeling, he placed his hands on the stone in front of him and bowed low. He heard the soft rumble of the lattice flexing open, then the rustle of her feathered robe as she approached.

The voice that came from above was slow and halting, speaking in cadences he hadn't used for a thousand years and more. "Thou art from the place to which I was sent."

"Yamato," he said, straightening from his bow. An old name for Japan, and one she might remember.

"Why hast thou come hither?"

Gone was the courtesy he remembered from the past, the elegant deference of a court lady. She had always shown exquisite manners, even though her adoptive father was a bamboo-cutter; the old man had wanted the best for her, and paid for it with the gold the people of the moon hid inside the stalks of bamboo he cut. She spoke now with confidence, directness, and cool unconcern, dismissing him with the informal pronoun employed with servants back then.

There was no reason she should remember him, with warmth or any other feeling. More than a thousand years had passed; if her thoughts dwelt on anyone from that time, it would not be the humble guardsman who carried her letters to and from the Emperor.

He feared, though, that the problem ran much deeper than that.

"I am Satake Nakamitsu," he said. The name tasted strange on his lips, after living for generations as Kemuriyama. But that name had only ever been a bitter joke: *smoking mountain*. A reminder of how he'd found himself in this state. "I was there when your people came to retrieve you. I took your final letter, and your gift for the Emperor—"

"I remember," she said, indifferent. "That tells me not why thou art here."

The words stuck in his throat. Not because he was rusty with the old ways of speaking, the formal pronouns and honorific verbs for a lady of her stature—but because after so long, after so much effort, he was finally here in front of her, and she did not care.

She made a disappointed noise at his silence, then turned to go.

Without thinking, he reached out and caught the edge of her feathered robe. It seared his hand like ice, but he held on and she halted. "Release me."

"The Emperor is dead."

She stood very still, not looking at him. "Then he drank not of the elixir I gave him."

"Without you, he had no wish to live forever. He ordered us to burn it atop the mountain that reached closest to the heavens." A mountain that still vented steam from time to time, which legend remembered as the smoke of that fire. Over the centuries, *fushi*—immortality—had changed to *Fuji*.

"But thou," she said, "still livest."

"Yes."

Now she turned to face him again, dragging the feathers of her robe from his cramped, aching fingers. "Why art thou here?"

He cradled the injured hand against his chest. "I gave my word to the Emperor. When he learned that I would not die, he begged me to carry his final message to you. I have struggled for longer than you know to fulfill that promise."

"Very well." She twitched her robe straight, as if shaking off some invisible dust he had pressed upon it. "What is the message?"

"I cannot convey it to you as you are now."

"Why not?"

"Because of the robe you wear."

Her hand stilled on the feathers. "What meanest thou?"

He'd watched her change, the moment they laid it across her shoulders. The sadness in her eyes had faded like mist in the sun; even the marks of tears upon her cheeks burned away, replaced by the full radiance of her people. The old bamboo-cutter and his wife had wailed, the guards had begged her not to leave…but she turned her back on them all, as if their voices were no more significant to her than the cries of birds.

She—who had once loved the Emperor so deeply, who had been the very soul of kindness and compassion—had ceased to care.

He said, "The woman the Emperor spoke of was Kaguya-hime, the shining child found in a stalk of bamboo. It is to her and her alone that I will give his final message."

"I am she."

"You are not."

"Thou wishest me to remove this robe," she said. For the first time, her voice rose from its bored indifference. "Thou wishest me to remember what passed during my time of exile— not the facts of it, but the *feelings*. Hast thou forgotten? That exile was my punishment. When they came to bring me home, that was absolution. And now thou wouldst bid me resume my penance, for the sake of a few paltry words."

None of them had ever said what her crime was. Not Kaguya-hime, nor those who came to retrieve her.

But he remembered how happy she had been. How much she loved the dear old bamboo-cutter and the woman she called "Mother." How eagerly she awaited each new letter from the Emperor, and how she labored over each brushstroke of her replies to him, wanting to give him as much joy as he brought her.

"I think," he said slowly, "that the true punishment was not your exile. A punishment is something one suffers, and your only suffering was the awareness that your happiness there could not last. No, Kaguya-hime—I believe the cruelest thing your people did was not sending you to Earth. It was placing that robe upon your shoulders, causing you to forget the man you had come to love."

"I have forgotten him not."

"You remember the man, yes—but not your love for him. Remove the robe, be as you were, and hear his final words."

"Love and death bring pain," she said. One hand stabbed upward, her finger pointing at the jewel of Earth in the sky above. "All three things belong there, in *thy* world. Not mine. I feel no pain now, nor wish to."

"And when was the last time you felt joy?"

Her hand faltered, her finger curling inward. She collected it to her chest, cradling it like a wounded bird, as he had cradled his frozen hand before. "Thou claimest thy words will bring me joy?"

"No," he admitted. "But if you remove your robe, you may remember the joy of the past. The joy which your own people have stolen from you."

She did not respond. Neither did she move. She merely stood, her breathing shallow and her eyes unblinking, until he rose and extended his hands. Even then she did not speak. But she lifted her chin, allowing him to reach the clasp at the base of her radiant throat.

The feathered robe floated down—and Kaguya-hime wept.

He knelt and waited, gaze trained on the jade-green stone of his prison's floor. He would wait as long as she needed. Grief was no less powerful for being suppressed a thousand years and more.

At last her voice came, barely louder than a gentle breeze. "What were his words for me?"

"He composed a poem." While gazing up at the moon during an interminable court party—but all such things had become interminable for the Emperor, after Kaguya-hime was gone. Squaring his shoulders, the man who had once served that Emperor recited:

> *If against my will*
> *I should have a long life in*
> *   this transient world,*
> *it is this moon at midnight*
> *that I no doubt will yearn for!*

With those words, his promise was fulfilled. He tensed, waiting, wondering. Hoping.

But nothing happened.

Only Kaguya-hime drawing a slow, shuddering breath, the sound of someone holding in further tears. His own eyes were dry. Disappointment had come often enough in his endless life—and he still had one hope left.

He waited for her to speak, assuming the long silence was Kaguya-hime struggling once more to regain her composure. But then, haltingly, she spoke.

> *In my memories*
> *of that world of yours that I*
> *   was forced to depart,*
> *oh, how I wish that there was*
> *one more meeting with you now.*

Words not for him, but for her lost love.

In one swift move Kaguya-hime caught up her feathered robe and cast it over the edge of the prison. It flared and seemed to float in the still air, then drifted away, toward the rapid approach of night.

"I thank you," Kaguya-hime said, and this time her voice was the one he remembered. "Your service to your Emperor is complete at last. As he is not here to reward you, hesitate not to ask it of me: What may I do in exchange for your gift?"

The man known as Kemuriyama, the man who had once been Satake Nakamitsu, pressed his forehead to the stone and said, "I beg you to help me die."

She knelt before him, her under-robe piling into soft, shimmering folds. "If you drank the elixir, then you should be able to choose the time of your death."

Her message to the Emperor had not made that clear. And even if it had—"I did not drink it."

One of his fellow guardsmen had suggested it: that *they* could take the elixir of life the Emperor had refused. Even if they shared it, the man reasoned, they would each live a long and prosperous life, if not an eternal one. Satake had killed him for his blasphemous presumption.

Such painful irony, much later, when he realized what breathing in the smoke of the fire had done to him.

Her flawless face settled into grave lines as he explained. When he was done, he said, "I do not know if you can kill me. Nothing has: not fire, nor water, nor the edge of a blade; not even lifeless space itself. But it was your people who made the elixir. If anyone can take this immortality from me, that person will be found here."

"Smoke," she mused, tilting her head to one side in a gesture he remembered. "You breathed it in…can you not breathe it out again?"

"If I could, then surely walking across the Moon would have done it."

A faint frown creased her smooth brow. "I cannot discern your meaning."

Because to her, the moon was a different place: not an airless rock floating in vacuum, but a city filled with jade towers like bamboo.

It was both. And perhaps the smoke from the elixir was also more than one thing: the air and particles of ash he had inhaled, and the power it had contained.

"I don't know how," he said.

She gazed thoughtfully into the distance. "Perhaps the message you bore kept it trapped within you. Now that you have spoken, the way is open."

He breathed in, then out, experimenting. It felt no different— save that he no longer carried the weight of an unfulfilled promise. Was that enough?

Breathe it out. His immortality; his attachment to life.

He stood and walked to the edge of the courtyard, lifting his chin to gaze upon the Earth. It had rotated so that East Asia was facing the Moon; he could just make out the archipelago of Japan, forming a sickle curve off the coast. By now Itō would be back there, bombarded with questions she could not answer. By now they'd opened his locker, found his explanation.

Perhaps some of them would understand. Itō wouldn't. She spoke mournfully of the long-term space programs, all the work in progress now whose fruition she wouldn't live to see. If someone offered her immortality, she would probably take it.

But human life was meant to be ephemeral. A poem in praise of a flower's brief glory, or the reflection of the moon in water.

He was tired of permanence. He was ready to fade.

Despite centuries of practice, composition still took effort, the patient counting of syllables and consideration of imagery. But his death poem came to him effortlessly, rising from deep within, where the smoke had lodged so many centuries ago.

> *The last spark is out:*
> *The skies above Mount Fuji*
> *Are finally clear.*

With his eyes fixed on the radiant jewel of Earth, he stepped off into the air.

Afterword

Like many academic disciplines, the field of folklore has had to wrestle with how to define itself and its object of study. What *is* folklore? Many of the definitions scholars have proposed over the decades invoke the concept of "tradition": traditional beliefs, traditional stories, traditional practices. But of course that only kicks the can down the road, because now you have to define what you mean by tradition—a question every bit as thorny as the one you started with.

My favorite answer comes, not from any academic folklorist, but from the composer Gustav Mahler: "Tradition is not the worship of ashes, but the preservation of fire." Instead of trying to provide a technical definition, it goes poetically to the notion of tradition as a *living thing*—something we keep alight by constantly providing it with new fuel, rather than insisting it remain unchanged, ossified, dead.

The grand tradition of fictional retellings seems to me an expression of Mahler's ideal. The story of Cinderella is not limited to Perrault's "Cendrillon" or the Grimms' "Aschenputtel" or any other fixed text; its fire keeps burning through all the iterations we make of it, from the classic 1950 Disney film to the non-fantastical *Ever After* (1998) to queer renditions that pair the heroine with a princess or make Cinderella male. Want to tell a Marxist version that argues with the entire notion of royalty and ends with Cinderella leading an army of transformed mice to decapitate the prince? Go right ahead. Although there was a stretch of time that folklorists believed they could borrow the methods of historical linguistics to work their way back to the "ur-text," the singular, original version from which all later variations sprang, the truth is that we've always been adapting and recombining our stories into new forms.

As for the other element of the title, that's my nod to the originally sacred character of some of the source material here. Mythology, to a folklorist, is not simply a catch-all term for old stories; it refers to narratives of a sacred nature, whose purpose is to explain how things came into existence, why the world works the way it does. Not everything in this book stems from myth; I've also ventured into epics and folktales (though not the familiar fairy tales of Western Europe; those are all in my collections *Monstrous Beauty* and *Never After: Thirteen Tales*). Some of them riff more on a concept or a character than the specific details of a plot. All of them, however, stand atop that foundation of tradition, the beliefs and stories passed down from one generation to the next.

I make absolutely *no* claim to be some kind of authoritative custodian of the fires referenced in this collection. As the range of geographic origins shows, I've reached well beyond the areas connected to my own heritage. Each story here simply represents a spark thrown off by something I read, which burned brightly enough in my mind to grow into something new. If I've piqued your interest anywhere, I hope you seek out the source—because that, too, is part of the preservation of fire. There may not be a singular, original version, but there is a central light being refracted through all the variations. And in that light, you too may find beauty and inspiration.

For notes on the individual stories, turn the page.

Story Notes

NOTES ON "THIS IS HOW"

Sometimes I can tell as soon as I finish drafting a story that I've got something good on my hands.

And then sometimes I finish and think, "welp, that's a thing," and only realize later that maybe it's actually one of my best pieces.

So it was with "This Is How." Which had an odd journey to the page, because of all things, it started with one of the bestiaries (monster manuals) from the *Pathfinder* role-playing game. I was looking through the various types of fey and came across the vilderavn, which I hadn't heard of before; it turned out to be based on a Danish creature more commonly called either a *valravn* ("raven of the slain," with the same first element as "valkyrie") or a *vilde valravn* (a "wild raven of the slain").

This hooked my attention because I thought a reformed vilderavn might make an intriguing love interest for the character I was playing in a game at the time. Since my subconscious is prone to fiddling around with ideas in multiple directions, it also sort of hived off into two partially-conjoined concepts for novels. And then one night, as I was on my way to bed, I got mugged by a *completely unrelated* approach to the character—and that's the one I ended up writing. (Though I wouldn't rule out the possibility that one of those other versions might also come into being someday.)

When I finished it, I wasn't sure if it even worked as a story. After some mulling and revision, I figured it was at least good enough to send around to markets. To my utter shock, *Strange Horizons* bought it—a magazine I'd been submitting to for literally seventeen years without success. When I re-read the story then, I found myself liking it a lot more than I remembered, and when it got published, it got more powerful responses from readers than any other piece of short fiction I'd written before then.

Which just goes to show that authors are not always very wise judges of their own work.

"This Is How" was originally published in *Strange Horizons* in September 2019.

NOTES ON "SERPENT, WOLF, AND HALF-DEAD THING"

If there's a pattern to the genesis of the stories in this collection, it's that they were inspired by my academic work somehow, or else by a throwaway comment someone else made.

This is one of the latter, and I can't even remember quite what the comment was. It was just something the writer Marissa Lingen said on her blog that made me think about the three offspring of Loki—the wolf Fenrir, the serpent Jormungandr, and the goddess Hel—not just as his children, but as siblings. Which I figured had to be one *truly* screwed-up family, given what happens with them all in mythology. And then, naturally, having thought of that, I had to write about it.

It started with the imprisonment of Loki, because that felt like something they would all have reactions to. But along the way, I remembered that Hel isn't really mentioned in the stories of Ragnarok, the epic battle that will be the "twilight of the gods." The dead she rules over are, and so are her siblings—but Hel herself just sort of vanishes from the picture. Which gave me what I needed to turn this from a sort of aimless "hey, they're siblings; what's up with that" bit of wandering into something with a destination.

Also, I should admit that the comments about the dead and living halves of Hel's face and how those affect her interaction with people owe something to how I depicted Hel when I played her in a live-action roleplaying game about the gods. (Not the one that had *me* as plot Macguffins; I ran that one rather than playing in it.) I decided on the fly that she only showed the living half of her face to people she liked…which was a very, very short list.

"Serpent, Wolf, and Half-Dead Thing" was originally published in *Bubble Off Plumb*, edited by K.G. Finfrock, Sarah Kalin, and Dan Kalin, in December 2018.

Notes on "The Waking of Angantyr"

This short story—like my novel of the same title—is the bastard child of my senior college thesis.

Said thesis was on weapons in Viking Age Scandinavia, and in the course of working on it, I both read a bunch of Norse sagas in translation, and took a semester of study in the Old Norse language itself. Which introduced me to a poem called "The Waking of Angantyr," in which a young woman named Hervor raises up the ghost of her father Angantyr to demand he give her his cursed sword Tyrfing. The material surrounding the versions I read gave me the distinct impression that she did this in order to get revenge for his death and those of his eleven brothers, so I went to great lengths to hunt down a copy of the saga it comes from—variously called *Hervor's Saga*, *The Saga of Hervor and Heiðrek*, or *The Saga of King Heiðrek the Wise*—so that I could read the rest of the story.

My 2023 novel *The Waking of Angantyr* came about because the saga turned out to be a disappointing mess in which Hervor does *not* get revenge, in part because one of the guys responsible is already dead and the other has his own saga to go get killed in. I wrote the novel to give myself the bloody tale of vengeance I felt I'd been promised. But before I did that, I wrote this story.

In fact, I wrote something like seven versions of this story, before I finally wound up with one that satisfied me. It's a bit of a challenging concept, since of course the revenge isn't in here; it's just about the confrontation with Angantyr's ghost, and I had to figure out how to make that feel like a self-contained thing. And somewhere along the line, the metrical and alliterative patterns of Norse poetry kind of infected the prose, to the point where one of the friends I asked to critique the current draft went through and started marking the scansion of the lines.

I should note that while it's generally my policy not to change my stories when I reprint them except where necessary to correct typos, this one is something of a double exception. Firstly, like the first draft of the novel *The Waking of Angantyr*, this story originally referred to the magic Hervor uses as *seidr* (aka *seiðr*, to give it its proper Norse spelling). In between then and now I've learned more about *seiðr*—enough to know that it has absolutely bugger-all to do with what I invented for my purposes. I changed the name to *drauðr* in the novel, and revised here to match. And second, the version that saw publication was not my final approved text, so the version reprinted here is that latter rather than the story as printed.

"The Waking of Angantyr" was originally published in the second issue of *Heroic Fantasy Quarterly*, in October 2009.

Notes on "Silence, Before the Horn"

It's no secret that the roleplaying games which have been a major hobby of mine since graduate school have often influenced my fiction in one way or another. In this case the influence is very tangential, but I want to acknowledge it nonetheless.

A friend of mine briefly ran an "avatar" game—one where all of our characters were actually ourselves, imported into the world of the story. The conceit was that we were all superheroes, but a government program to decommission supers had suppressed our powers and our memories of our real identities. The game began with us being re-activated and starting to recover our abilities.

My friend knew that I liked swords and fencing, so her idea for me was that my powers were derived from a magical sword I bore, and she'd tentatively imagined a backstory for it that had something to do with the Lady of the Lake in Arthurian legend. I told her that since a lot of my ancestry is Scandinavian, I liked the idea of making it more of a valkyrie thing instead, and she agreed.

That night, after the session had ended, my subconscious said *why not both?*

This had zero effect on my character, and the game only lasted one or two sessions anyway. But I sat down and immediately knocked out a draft of a flash-fiction piece in which the Lady of the Lake *is* a valkyrie—one who, like some of her sisters, was trying to retire from her duties. The return of Arthur and the rallying of the *einherjar*, Odin's army of slain heroes, linked up with each other to tie the whole thing together in the inevitable future of Ragnarok.

In some ways I think this may be the most perfect story I've ever written. Not the same thing as saying it's the *best*; at a mere 379 words, there's not a lot of room in it for substance. (These notes are longer than the story itself.) But there's honestly nothing in it that I would change, not even down to the commas: it is exactly what I want it to be. It may also be the closest thing I've written to a prose poem, though I feel singularly unqualified to judge what does and does not qualify for that descriptor.

"Silence, Before the Horn" was originally published in the first issue of *Jabberwocky*, in July 2005.

Notes on "Daughter of Necessity"

I owe Diana Wynne Jones thanks for this story twice over. First, because her novel *Fire and Hemlock* is the book that made me decide I wanted to be a writer; and second, because of a comment she once made about Penelope.

When I heard that Jones had passed away, I embarked on a memorial project of reading and posting about all of her works. The last title I tackled was the recently-published *Reflections*, which collects various essays of hers. In the piece "The Heroic Ideal: A Personal Odyssey," she comments that Penelope, like Odysseus, uses her mind to outwit her opponents—but her trickery is of a passive kind, using the weaving and unweaving of the funeral shroud to stall for time. Which immediately made me wonder if that could somehow be an active bit of strategy instead.

It didn't take long at all for my brain to point out that, for the Greeks, textiles and fate were intimately linked.

If memory serves, I wrote the entirety of this story while sitting in an airport waiting for a flight. I'd been teaching for a month as a part of Duke TIP (Talent Identification Program), running gifted twelve- and thirteen-year-olds through a crash course on science fiction and fantasy writing; the logistics of getting me to the airport afterward meant I was dropped off there something like four hours before I needed to be. I sat in the concourse and fell down research rabbit holes of ancient weaving technology and the names of Penelope's suitors, making on-the-fly decisions about verb tenses (narrating in the future tense is often clunky and obtrusive, but in this case it made sense), and soon had a story I was very quietly pleased with.

So pleased, in fact, that I wound up doing something I almost never do: I read the story at a convention, even though I hadn't sold it yet. One person who was in the audience for that went from not knowing my work at all to being a staunch fan, just on the basis of this piece, so I feel justified in thinking of it as one of my better stories ever.

And its publication history supports that interpretation. It was originally published on Tor.com in October 2014; they later reprinted it in *Some of the Best from Tor.com 2014* (January 2015) and again in *Worlds Seen in Passing: Ten Years of Tor.com Short Fiction* (September 2018). It was also reprinted in *Nevertheless, She Persisted,* ed. Mindy Klasky, in August 2017.

Notes on "Your Body, My Prison, My Forge"

Writers differ widely on how they approach the writing process. In my case, my first draft usually looks a fair bit like the final version of the story; if it comes out truly badly, that tends to mean the story concept itself isn't very good, and I don't bother revising it. But every so often I'll take a run at something, face-plant, and try again—and so it was with this tale.

Part of the problem was, of the pieces I knew I'd be putting into this collection, this was one of the last ones I wrote. And that meant I couldn't help but think of it in context with all the others. Should it be in first person? Third person? Name the protagonist, or leave her nameless until the end? Everything I could think of, I'd already done, and I chafed at the idea that it would sound too much like "Daughter of Necessity" or "Serpent, Wolf, and Half-Dead Thing" or "Centuries of Kings." I wrote a third-person draft that named Metis outright, but it just felt lifeless and uninteresting. How could I make it stand out?

I don't remember which idea came first: writing it in first person, direct address (where the "I" of the narrator is speaking to some "you" within the story), or the body horror answer to "where is Metis getting the materials to forge weapons and armor for Athena?" As body horror goes, of course, this is quite mild… but since it's something I almost never touch on in my fiction, that in combination with the point of view gave me a fresh angle from which to approach the concept.

As for the concept itself, like many of my retellings, it was born from me asking a question of the source. Athena springs from the head of Zeus not only fully grown but armed and armored—so where do those things come from? That led me backward to the story of Zeus swallowing Metis, and thence to the notion of her being the one who forged these things for her daughter.

"Your Body, My Prison, My Forge" was published in issue #124 of the Canadian magazine *On Spec*, in July 2023.

Notes on "For the Fairest"

Way back in 2004, I went on a kick of writing flash fiction—stories under either 1000 or 500 words, depending on whose definition you're using. The vast majority of the resulting pieces were based on fairy tales (and wound up collected in *Never After: Thirteen Twists on Familiar Tales*), but in an attempt to branch out ever so slightly, I wrote one inspired by Greek mythology.

And also by fanfiction. Cassandra Clare, best known these days for the Mortal Instruments series, wrote a piece of fan-fiction after the release of the movie *The Fellowship of the Ring* called "The Very Secret Diaries," which gave a tongue-in-cheek look at how different members of the Fellowship viewed their adventures and their companions. Because Legolas was played by Orlando Bloom, each of his entries included a notation that he was "still the prettiest." So when Bloom also played Paris in the 2004 film *Troy*…it wasn't even a leap. What if Paris, upon being given an apple inscribed "for the fairest," decided to keep it for himself?

(By the way, the Greek section of this collection is totally out of order, both in terms of date of composition and in-story chronology. Technically it ought to be "Your Body, My Prison, My Forge" for the birth of Athena, then "For the Fairest" with the Judgment of Paris, then "The Wives of Paris" for the aftermath of that judgment and the Trojan War, then "Daughter of Necessity" for the return of Odysseus after the war. But the conventional wisdom of anthologies and collections holds that you should put one of your strongest pieces up front—and while this little piece of flash does amuse me, in a contest between it and "Daughter of Necessity," Penelope wipes the floor with Paris.)

"For the Fairest" was published in the first issue of *Son and Foe*, in December 2005.

Notes on "The Wives of Paris"

This…was not the story I meant to write.

For several years after I moved to California I belonged to a local writers' group. At one of the meetings, a friend of mine talked about a story she was thinking of writing, that would be about both the Trojan War and Heinrich Schliemann's excavation of Troy in the nineteenth century, with ghosts and other cool things involved. Sadly, I don't think she ever wrote it—but something she said during that conversation made me start speculating about what would have happened if Paris had awarded the golden apple to a different goddess.

That much remained accurate. Had you asked me to describe the story then, however, I would have told you it was going to be lyrical, poetic, as lush and mythic in tone as I could manage. You can, if you look closely, still see that plan in the first sentence of the story.

…but then I wrote a second sentence, and the plan wobbled. A third sentence, and it tottered. At the fourth sentence it fell over completely, and the story declared at it was going to be *snarky*.

I could have resisted, I suppose. But when a story establishes its voice that clearly, trying to force it to be something else rarely ends well. And although this tale has a wildly different feeling compared to "Daughter of Necessity," they share both an exploration of alternate futures, and a special place in my heart.

It was published in the "0.1" issue of *Mythic Delirium* in July 2013, and then reprinted in the *Mythic Delirium* anthology, ed. Mike and Anita Allen, in November 2014.

Notes on "The *Me* of Perfect Sight"

I have slightly compulsive tendencies, and so I had the goal—which ended up getting changed; more on that in a few pages—of having three stories for each of the regional groupings this collection was coalescing into. Which meant I needed a third Near Eastern story.

For a while it was a close race whether I'd wind up writing about Humbaba (the giant defeated by Gilgamesh and Enkidu in

The Epic of Gilgamesh, and featured in a recently-discovered missing fragment from that tale), the descent of Inanna into the under-world, or the *me*—the "decrees" that sort of embody different concepts in physical form. My husband and I had made fruitful use of the *me* in a live-action roleplaying game we ran, making the *me* of kingship and the *me* of ascent from the underworld Macguffins for various deities to strive after, and I liked the story of how Inanna got Enki drunk and convinced him to hand them all over.

But the actual story morphed through a bunch of different shapes before it settled into this one. Initially I thought I might call it "The *Me* of the Theft of *Me*" and link it to how Prometheus stole fire from Mount Olympus; it also briefly flirted with the idea of instead being about Inanna's *sukkal* Ninshubur (not named here), who also features in "The Descent of Inanna." The Promethean concept didn't work out, but I liked the comparative mythology it brought in—something that also shows up in "The Wives of Paris"—so, despite the fact that I quite enjoy Inanna's role in these events, the story I wrote wound up focusing on Enki.

"The *Me* of Perfect Sight" was originally published in issue #58 *NewMyths*, in March 2022.

NOTES ON "THE GOSPEL OF NACHASH"

This is not an Onyx Court story, but it owes its existence to my research for that series.

While I was working on *A Star Shall Fall*, which is set in the eighteenth century, I happened to have dinner with a college friend of my husband's, Devin McLachlan, who had become an Episcopal minister—i.e. part of the Anglican Communion, i.e. connected with the Church of England. I took the opportunity to pick his brain on the question of what eighteenth-century Anglican theologians might have thought about faeries, and this morphed into a discussion of how new astronomical discoveries in that era caused those theologians to debate 1) whether there was life on other planets, 2) if so, whether that life was touched by original sin, and 3) if so, whether they had been redeemed by Christ's crucifixion, or whether they would need their own Messiahs to redeem them.

Whereupon I said, "That makes me want to write about a faerie Christ."

The resulting story owes a great deal to the assistance of my friend Jessica Hammer, who guided me through Jewish midrashim regarding questions like "where did the wives of Cain and Abel come from" and "what are the nephilim" and other puzzles of early scripture. What I wound up aiming to do was fill in some of those gaps by use of faeries, and also fill in some gaps of faerie lore by use of scripture. I owe Devin, Jessica, and Yonatan Zunger copious thanks for their assistance in helping to make that happen.

I'm not sure where in the process the prose style got decided. For various reasons, the early seventeenth-century English of the King James Version has been enshrined in the public conscious-ness as "biblical language"—but it's not what you would call the normal approach for fiction today. I am extremely grateful that the editor Mike Allen likes unusual, even baroque prose styles, because if he hadn't bought it, I'm not sure who would have.

"The Gospel of Nachash" was originally published in *Clockwork Phoenix 3*, edited by Mike Allen, in July 2010.

NOTES ON "SALT FEELS NO PAIN"

Somewhat embarrassingly, I'm not entirely sure I remember what prompted me to write this story. I *think* it was for a class I took in graduate school; certainly it dates to the first semester of my third year, which is when the course I associate it with happened. But if I did write the story for the class, I foolishly cut the file from that folder (instead of copying it), so there's no surviving proof linking the two. Since I'm not entirely sure how this would have matched with the topic of the course, I may be entirely imagining the connection.

But I do remember the general thought process behind the

story. The liberal evangelical blogger "Slacktivist" (Fred Clark) discussed at one point the story of Sodom and Gomorrah, where the patriarch Lot gave hospitality to two angels who visited in disguise. When the men of Sodom demanded he bring out his guests so they could "know" them (read: rape them), Lot offered up his two virgin daughters instead.

Like Clark, I have difficulty seeing anything virtuous in Lot's actions, that should qualify him to be spared from the destruction of the city. Sure, it's important to protect your guests, but at the cost of some innocent girls instead? I think I got my wires crossed, though, in what follows after; I had it in my head that Lot then decides to have sex with his daughters, but looking back at the actual text, Lot's daughters get their father passing-out drunk and then rape him in turn so they can have children. This entire mess is why I wound up writing a story about his unnamed wife, and running with the idea that she purposefully turns to look back at the city, knowing it will destroy her—but feeling that is preferable to remaining with her family.

"Salt Feels No Pain" was originally published in the thirteenth and final issue of *Paradox*, in May 2009.

NOTES ON "AT THE HEART OF EACH PEARL LIES A GRAIN OF SAND"

I didn't actually have to write this story.

But…the numbers kept not lining up. My stories initially divided fairly neatly into Greco-Roman, Germanic, and what at the time I was calling the Near Eastern and Asian categories (because the latter used to have an Indian story in it), and as I said before, I was aiming for three of each. Before I came up with "The *Me* of Perfect Sight," however, I wrote "This Is How," which put the Germanic category up to four, and then I wound up with four Asian ones, too, and even though there was *absolutely nothing wrong with this*—I had enough material to satisfy my self-imposed minimum threshold for a collection—it bugged me that the sections were getting so far out of balance with each other. So if you wonder why this book, coming out in 2024, contains stories from all the way back in 2005, well, this is why it took so long for me to publish it. I wanted four stories for each section, dangit.

This one is the reason I finally changed the term for this group of stories from "Near Eastern" to "West Asian" (which also makes a tidier parallel with "East Asian"). Although the former term still sees some legacy use in discussing ancient times—i.e. the periods from which the previous three stories are drawn—the source material for this one is more recent: the famous *One Thousand and One Nights*, specifically the tale "The Porter and the Three Ladies of Baghdad." It's a convoluted piece with (as is common for that collection) tales nested within it, but on reaching the end, I was struck by the fact that the third lady's story is never told. Why not? What could her story be? Nothing I could come up (except science fiction, which isn't so much my speed) with would stand out among the weirdness of the other tales…which then wound up being my answer. But the part about how wondrous it is for her husband to actually keep his promise? That part, I didn't plan; it emerged along with the story.

"At the Heart of Each Pearl Lies a Grain of Sand" was originally published in *The Sunday Morning Transport*, in April 2023.

NOTES ON "CENTURIES OF KINGS"

File this one under "stories that came out of my academic studies." During graduate school I took a rather disappointing class on Japanese fantasy—disappointing because the teacher very clearly liked a literary mode she called "psychodrama," in which it's left ambiguous whether something supernatural is going on, or whether the main character is delusional, or whether it's all just a metaphor. That was the vast majority of what we read, and all the very blatantly fantastical stuff in Japanese literature more or less got swept under the rug.

But we did start with Royall Tyler's collection of translated folklore, *Japanese Tales*, and for one of the assignments I persuaded the professor to let me write a short story based on one of those tales, that of the *kitsune* (fox spirit) Tamamo-no-Mae. Somewhere in the course of my research I wound up connecting it to some related stories from China and even India—but sadly, whatever book I got that from is buried in the depths of the Indiana University library system, its title long since forgotten. (Which is also why the pinyin romanization of "Pao Si" is a complete guess: in the original version of the story it was "Pao Sze," and I've failed to figure out which romanization system that came from, since it seems to partake of two different ones. Chinese linguistics not being my specialty, I did my best.)

Anyway, the conceit of the story was that the fox spirit in those different tales was the same one throughout. It got me a good grade in the class, and then I turned around and sold it, which is pretty much the most useful thing I got out of taking that course—since it certainly didn't teach me anything about the kind of fantasy I'm interested in.

"Centuries of Kings" was originally published in *Neverland's Library*, edited by Rebecca Lovatt and Roger Bellini, in April of 2014.

NOTES ON "THE OLD WOMAN AND THE TEA"

The game I mentioned before, the one my husband and I ran that used the *me* as a plot macguffin, wound up spawning a story rather more directly.

It was a special side event for an ongoing game set in the World of Darkness—which, for those who aren't familiar with it, is an urban fantasy setting where lots of supernatural creatures exist and also everything is kind of dystopian and grim. Because of that, my husband and I decided that during the Cultural Revolution, the Red Guard didn't merely destroy religious sites and objects; hunters among them succeeded in killing many of the Chinese gods. One of the few to survive was Meng Po/Old Lady

Meng, who's responsible for making sure souls forget their previous lives before they're reincarnated.

In the game Meng Po made the hunters forget her so thoroughly, it caused her problems afterward; nobody who met her could remember that meeting or anything that happened in it. (Fixing that was one of the plots we created for that player to engage with.) Whether that happens to the Meng Po you see in this story is beyond the scope of the tale itself; I just realized one day that I could make a little flash tale out of the original background concept.

What she serves to the souls before reincarnation is variously referred to in English as a water, a tea, or a soup; I went with "tea" here because I honestly couldn't resist the random play on Hemingway's famous title.

"The Old Woman and the Tea" was originally published in *Daily Science Fiction*, in July 2021.

Notes on "Ghost and Fox"

My friend Larry Hammer is somewhat responsible for two of the stories in this collection. This is the first.

It came about because he had on multiple occasions mentioned a certain work of Qing Dynasty literature by Pu Songling, *Liáozhāi zhìyì*, a selection of which is available from Penguin Classics under the title *Strange Tales from a Chinese Studio*. *Liáozhāi* is sort of a literary folktale collection, published in 1740. The stories translated in John Minford's 2006 version range all over, but feature a lot of instances of fox spirits and/or ghosts getting involved with mortal men. The one that inspired this piece, commonly titled "Lotus Fragrance"—which is the name of the fox spirit in question— struck me as kind of a transdimensional tale of happy polyamory: a ghost and a fox spirit who start out as rivals but eventually both find ways to return as humans so they can safely be with the man they love.

The story here differs from the original in a few key respects.

In Pu Songling's version, the ghost knows who she is immediately upon possessing the body of the recently deceased young woman, and the fox spirit has no involvement with arranging her return to life. But since I liked the arc of the fox initially being hostile to the ghost, but eventually warming to her, I tweaked the specifics— and amped up the idea that the fox and the ghost are not simply friends joined through their shared affection for the man, but actively come to love one another.

"Ghost and Fox" was published in the anthology *Shapers of Worlds II*, edited by Edward Willett, in November 2021.

Notes on "Speak to the Moon"

I mentioned before that Larry Hammer is responsible for inspiring two of the stories in this collection. This is the second one.

And it all started with a blog post. In discussing "The Tale of the Bamboo-Cutter," he questioned the entire coda in which the emperor disposes of the elixir of life by asking some of his warriors to burn it atop a mountain. Did they really follow through? Did it work? What happens if you inhale the smoke? Does it turn you into a monster?

He floated a bunch of different alternate possibilities, and while none of them quite clicked in my head, they immediately instilled in me the desire to write *something* riffing off that tale. As with my *Mahabharata* story "Sankalpa" (but for far less obvious reasons), it took me ages to finally turn it into a story—about eight years, in fact. And to my surprise, what finally made it cohere was the random injection of some science fiction.

I'm not even sure what made that angle come into my head. I write virtually nothing one could call SF; the closest I'd come before this was probably "The Genius Prize" (my kaiju vs. mecha story, collected in *Down a Street That Wasn't There*), whose connection to Actual Science is made of string cheese. But as soon as I thought of an immortal man fostering the Japanese space program in the hopes of finding the moon people so he can finally let go of his eternal life, the story started rolling. Who was I to argue with that?

I owe substantial thanks to my friend Erin Smith, the NASA scientist who's assisted me with other space- and astronomy-related research. We spent a great deal of time discussing not just what the effects of vacuum would be on an immortal, but how plausible it is that Japan would launch its own manned mission from Tanegashima rather than piggybacking off an existing manned flight program. The answer is, not very; the expertise needed for that is so specialized, with such high risks, that it's wiser to work with existing teams than to try and spin up your own. But given the nature of the tale, I decided to keep the focus on Japan throughout.

"Speak to the Moon" was originally published in *The Magazine of Fantasy and Science Fiction*, aka *F&SF*, in their March/April 2021 issue—and, like my sale of "This Is How" to *Strange Horizons*, was the culmination of many years of persistent effort. Never let anyone tell you that just because a market has declined to purchase the first fifty-three things you've sent them, there's no point in trying for a fifty-fourth time!

About the Author

About Book View Café

Book View Café Publishing Cooperative (BVC) is an author-owned cooperative of professional writers, publishing in a variety of genres such as fantasy, romance, mystery, and science fiction.

BVC authors include New York Times and USA Today bestsellers; Nebula, Hugo, and Philip K. Dick Award winners; World Fantasy Award and Campbell Award nominees; and winners and nominees of many other publishing awards.

Since its debut in 2008, BVC has gained a reputation for producing high-quality e-books, and is now bringing that same quality to its print editions.